The *D* in DRAMA

Christiana Harrell

Photography:

Edited By: Christina Cosse'

Email the author: wordsRmylife86@yahoo.com

First Edition

Visit: christianaharrell.com

ISBN-13: 978-1479214914

ISBN-10: 1479214914

Dedication:

This book is for every fan who wanted more of these characters. I did this for you ☺

Artist Mentioned in this book:

Shaky Shawn
Jas'mine Garfield
Country
Temper
B. Steady

Table of Contents

CHAPTER 1

Rose

"Hello," I answered the phone happy to hear from Emmitt.

"What you doing baby girl?" He said through the phone and his deep voice sent chills up my spine and put an automatic smile on my face.

"Nothing, I was laying here waiting for you to call." I said through my smile as I lay across my bed, flat on my stomach with the back of my legs curled up.

"Sorry about that love the coach kept us kind of late tonight."

"It's cool," I said as I adjusted the phone on my ear and commenced to play with my nails, "after three years of this I think I'm used to it by now. You'll be going pro soon and be one of the best quarterbacks in the league, and then you can just pay to see me whenever you want." I smiled.

1

"Yeah, so umm you start school tomorrow huh?"

"Yeah and I'm so excited! I'm finally a junior. I can't believe I'll have one more year and then I can come and be with you." I said as more matter of fact than as a suggestion.

He hesitated before speaking, "you know I was thinking…"

"Thinking what?" I placed a pause on my fidgeting hands at those dreadful words.

"Maybe we should test new waters," He swallowed, "I mean with me being all the way in Texas and you in Louisiana I really don't see us maintaining our relationship for another year." He said with ease.

"Excuse me?" I sat up in my bed to make sure I was hearing him right.

"Rose please don't make me repeat it. I just think it'll be easy this way and then we won't have to deal with traveling and arguing because we miss each other."

"I don't think I understand what you're trying to say to me…."

"Rose," He took a breath "look, you still have a lot ahead of you with graduation and…"

I cut him off, "are you saying I'm too young for you now?"

"That's not what I'm saying; don't put words in my mouth…"

"Then make your fucking point already and stop rambling. If you don't want to be with me anymore Emmitt say you don't want to be with me."

"Rose I'm sorry I just don't see how we can work. I'm not cut out for the long distance thing anymore."

"We've been doing this for three years without a problem now suddenly your back at school for two weeks and you can't see how we can work?! Who is she?"

He huffed into the phone.

"You know what, it doesn't even matter. Its funny how two weeks ago I was all that you needed and blah blah bullshit, I guess you were just saying all that to get me to give up the pussy one last time before you hauled ass to Texas! FUCK YOU EMMITT! FUCK YOU!"

Tears welled up in my eyes as I became overwhelmed with emotion. I didn't even let him get another word out. I just hung up the phone and tossed my face into my pillow. I was not the girl that got broken up with. I never believed that I was just some silly girl with a dream that my college boyfriend was actually going to be faithful to me and never leave me. I believed from the bottom of my heart that Emmitt loved me and only me because we had a real history. I knew his entire family and he knew mine. We grew up together and started to date once I was in high school. He was my first and I thought he would be my last. He always told me that I was the most beautiful girl in the world and I believed him. I fucking believed him.

My mother rushed into my room after hearing the profanities I had thrown around so freely as if she wasn't there. "Have you lost your mind in…" She stopped in her tracks as she realized I was crying

3

nonstop and paying no mind to her scold. She walked over to my bed and sat down on the edge, placing her hand on my back, rubbing it in an attempt to soothe my jerking body. "Rose baby what's the matter?"

"He …broke…up…with…me…" I continued to cry into my pillow.

"Emmitt? He did what?"

I felt as though I couldn't breathe as my mother rubbed my back. "This hurts so bad…" my voice cracked.

"I know baby. I know." she continued to rub. My mother gave me a free pass for using bad words after discovering that my first love had given me a taste of heart ache. She left me alone to cry all night.

The instant that the sun came up I wanted all of it to be a dream. I was supposed to be the girl he kept because I was his high school sweetheart. I was the girl he married and had kids with. I was the girl that collected evidence of his cheating ass years down the line so I could ruin his life and take his bitch ass for everything he had.

I reached for my cell phone and it started to ring in my hand. It was my best friend Akeisha. Akeisha and I had been friends since the seventh grade. I met her the second week of school when my mother chose to go on a date versus picking me up from school, so I had to ride the school bus. I stood out front staring at the line of yellow buses not sure who to ask about which one I had to ride. Akeisha saw my confused expression and asked me if I was lost. When I turned to look at her my first thought was 'wow she's big' but she was the first person who was nice to me at the new school. It turned out that

4

she and I lived in the same neighborhood so we had to ride the same bus. We had been close ever since. I told her all my secrets and she told me hers.

A lot of people thought of us as an odd pair because we looked completely opposite, but that didn't bother me at all. I honestly never felt that Akeisha was as unattractive as people made her out to be. She looked like a chocolate cabbage patch doll minus the rope stranded hair. Akeisha had really thin hair, so she usually kept it in braids unless there was a dance then she'd pull out the good weave.

"Hey girl," I said groggily into the phone.

"Hey girl nothing, why are you still sleeping," Akeisha's raspy voice asked concerned. I yawned and rolled over with the phone to my ear, "I don't feel like getting up."

"We have school today and we're late. Get up it's the FIRST day!" she yelled into my ear and I moved the phone.

"Emmitt broke up with me last night." I said completely disregarding her scolding.

"What?!"

"Yep, he wants to 'test new waters' aka he found a new, older bitch and he's done with little old me."

"Girl fuck that nigga, you are beautiful. You can have anybody you want."

I poked out my bottom lip, "but I don't want anybody I want Emmitt."

The pain I felt before I slept the night before started to conjure itself up again inside my body again.

"Get out of the bed and I'll be there in a minute so we can go to school, maybe being around other people will make you feel better. You're about to be seventeen Rose; it's not the end of the world and besides it's not like you were a complete angel throughout y'all entire relationship; need I bring up the revenge lay with Corey?"

"Oh gawd please don't bring that up. It was so not worth it. I'm glad he didn't tell anyone about that."

"Now get up before I start reminding you of some other disloyal things you did every time Emmitt hurt your feelings," Akeisha threatened.

Akeisha and I hung up. She was right. I pulled myself from the bed and walked over to my closet to pull out my uniform. Even though I felt like shit I didn't have to look it. I dressed and accessorized with gold bracelets, a cross pendant, and the diamond stud earrings that Emmitt just so happened to buy me before he left. I shook my head at the earrings but put them in my ears anyway.

Akeisha pulled up blowing the horn on her little raggedy 92 *Honda* and my mom burst into my room.

"You're ghetto ass friend is outside. Why on Earth do you hang with that girl?" she asked folding her arms across her chest.

"She's cool people." I responded while brushing my hair.

"Cool people? She's ugly and loud. You probably hang with her to make yourself look prettier than what you already are."

"Mom!" I yelled.

6

"Mom nothing, I'm grown and I don't have to sugarcoat anything."

"I grabbed my purse and my book bag and walked pass my mother, kissing her on the cheek, "I'll see you later mean lady."

"Uh huh," She stood with her arms still folded

I grabbed my door keys from the coffee table by our front door and hopped into the car with Akeisha. My mother peeped out of the window as we pulled off.

"You're mother can't stand me," Akeisha said.

"That's not true." I lied and we rolled on to school. I admired the scenery on the way as I rode. I loved New Orleans, even though it was the worse in crime and climbing up there in number with aids, it was still home and nobody understood the people there better than the natives themselves.

We pulled up to school and parked in the back of the student parking lot. I waved at Akeisha and headed to my first class.

Snapps

It was love at first sight as this fresh face graced my presence. I was sitting in the back with my head down as my history teacher lectured. That class was so damn boring and it was only the first day. How you could manage to make an entire class yawn from a syllabus alone was beyond me. When Rose walked in I could have sworn I saw a bright light. She was 5'6", her light brown hair fell past her shoulders

7

and around her face, surrounding her plump pink lips and green eyes, just a bad ass redbone. She was that intimidating kind of beautiful that instantly made you insecure about yourself and had you questioning if her attraction would be nothing more than trouble because of everyone else that would have no choice, but to notice her. Ma had it all. I thought I was dreaming. She was going in slow motion in my mind with her clean, white, perfectly starched button down and plaid skirt that was short enough to show that she was sexy and long enough to show she had class. I sat up in my seat, wondering what her voice sounded like. She sat in the middle of the room and joined in on the lecture. I watched her as she dug through her backpack for a pen and notebook. She was graceful with everything that she did as she pushed her hair behind her ear and pulled out paper and pen to begin her late notes.

I watched her the entire period wondering how it was possible that I had never seen her or didn't know who she was. I tore a slip of paper from my notebook and eased it over to my friend Lexi.

Lexi was one of the few studs in the school that I was cool with. She was real laid back and for that reason alone bitches fell at her feet. She was short, slim and she wore her hair in long braids that she of course had done by some random chick from school who was trying to get in wherever she could fit in. She didn't have to dribble a ball or pretend to be harder than she was to get play; she was just a slick ass nigga and a pretty one at that and I didn't call many studs pretty and I definitely never said it to her out loud, but she made it an effort to call me pretty boy every chance she got. I sat up and watched as she unfolded the paper to respond to my curiosity.

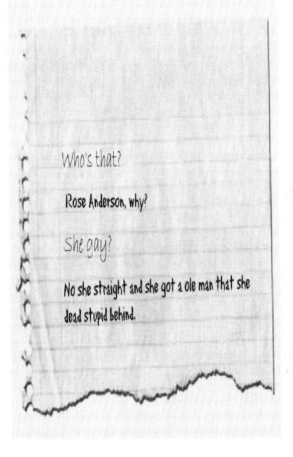

Who's that?

Rose Anderson, why?

She gay?

No she straight and she got a ole man that she dead stupid behind.

I balled up the slip of paper and tossed it in my bag, shaking my head. I really didn't care that she was straight and had a man, she was beautiful and I wanted her like I had never wanted anything or anybody in my life. I stared at her until the bell rang for our next period. I stood to watch witch direction she was going in and it just so happened to be the same one as me, so I paced five steps behind her. She walked into my next class and sat her bag down by a chair then walked out. I assumed she was going to the restroom since she stopped by the teacher for a second. I took a place at the back of the class again and watched her empty seat.

Fifteen minutes had gone by and nature was calling. I raised my hand and the teacher motioned for me to go and use the restroom, he knew I wasn't listening anyway. Most of my teachers never gave me my much of a hard time because I was top of my class when it came to grades. I was ready for college already, because nothing I learned posed a challenge for me.

I grabbed the hall pass and sprinted out the door to the restroom. People were roaming the hall, as I ran through. I had to go bad. Dudes looked at me stupid as I entered the girl's restroom. I had been going to school with most of these same cats since elementary and they still seemed shocked when they saw me walk into the ladies restroom to piss; fucking idiots. Just because I wore men's clothing didn't make me a man, now if I walked in the men's restroom, they'd all be behind me, staring like a bunch of fucking vultures, giggling like bitches, because I got a pussy between my legs. Once I was inside the restroom, I stepped into a stall and squatted to relieve myself, making sure not to touch the seat. I wiped and then flushed the toilet with my foot. I never touched the handle no telling what went on in public restrooms, public anything for that matter. I stepped out to wash my hands and I heard sobbing coming from one of the other stalls. I washed, rinsed, and dried, before knocking on the door, where the noise was coming from.

"Hey you ok in there?" I asked moving closer to the door.

"Yes, I'm fine."

"Don't sound like it ma. You want to talk about it?"

"Not really." Her voice echoed off the walls.

"I think you should, you might feel better."

"Is that right Dr. Phil?"

"Look I'm just tryna help, you the dumbass sitting in a stall balling like a bitch."

The door to the restroom stall swung open and there stood Rose with bloodshot red eyes. She had tissue in her hand and it was obvious that she had been running her hands through her hair from the way it stuck up. She looked as though she jumped straight out of bed and into a car without so much as brushing her teeth, compared to her sharp appearance earlier.

"Who the fuck are you calling a bitch?"

"Man calm down, you got smart with me first and I was just being nice and I'm not usually nice."

Rose pushed past me and went over to the sink to flush her face with water. She stood to dry it and then turned back to me.

"I'm sorry Snapps."

She knew my name, I thought to myself. Everyone called me Snapps because I was known for going off on a motherfucka. I preferred Snapps anyway because my mom had to be smoking dope when she named me Sasha Adams, which was some girly ass shit, maybe if she had known she was carrying a baby stud, she would have reconsidered.

"You're in my history and math class right?" Rose asked.

"Yea"

"Did the teacher send you to look for me?"

"No I had to piss."

"Oh…" she sounded disappointed.

"You ready to tell me what or who got you like this?"

"My boyfriend broke up with me last night. I've been crying since. He wants to 'test the waters'. I've been repeating that stupid shit over and over to myself," she wiped her eyes, "he's probably fucking some bitch on his campus as we speak, but I guess I should have seen that coming being with someone four years older than me. I wouldn't want to be twenty at a junior prom either."

"Fuck that nigga ma. He really isn't worth crying over. Any real nigga can see what your worth and I'm not saying that because you're beautiful. I've just been paying attention to you."

"Really for two whole class periods huh?" She laughed.

"You had to have been paying attention to me too if you knew already."

"I'm just observant." she said through stuffed nostrils.

"But back to my point. I've heard about all these dudes tryna get at you, but you don't budge. You stay too true to that lame."

"Yea well, not anymore. He doesn't want me."

"If you ask me you still being true, you sitting in the restroom stall crying, when there's a whole world out there full of people who'll do anything to be with you."

"I guess you're right, my best friend told me the same thing." she sniffed.

Rose turned back toward the mirror, rubbing her hand over her hair and checking her face. She applied lip gloss to her full lips then puckered them. I wanted to be in front stealing a kiss. I wanted to touch her to console her, pull her into me, and make her forget him. I watched in amazement as she transformed, pushing her hair back into place and dabbing her eyes with tissue, before flushing her face with cold water. Rose turned to me and smiled and I smiled back.

She and I walked back to class together and exchanged numbers. I sat at the back of the class looking at her as she held her head down, wondering if texting her at that moment would make me look pitiful. I honestly really didn't care. I pulled out my phone beneath my desk and sent her a text.

Rose smiled and placed her phone inside her bag. It was nice to see her smile. Now I was looking forward to lunch.

Rose wasn't in my next three classes, so they went by slowly because I watched the clock tick tock.

When the bell rang for lunch I grabbed all my things and ran to find Lexi. They had not assigned us lockers yet, so I couldn't just find her at hers. Lexi was heading in my direction from her fifth period class. "What we eating today pretty boy?" Lexi said.

"Pizza, follow me."

"Follow you where? I'm the one that drove today unless the pizza flying to us." she laughed.

"No we're eating with that girl I asked you about and her friend."

"Oh Rose," she gave half a smile, "nigga you just saw the girl and now y'all kickin' it?"

"I talked to her in class."

"You don't waste no time," Lexi laughed and I tooted my lips up and ignored her. "Man that girl is straight, you wasting your time and even if she does give you a chance, you just need to beat and run."

"I'm not you gigolo."

"I'm just saying," she shrugged her shoulders and continued to walk behind me to the parking lot.

Rose was standing exactly where she said she would with her friend. She smiled and waved as Lexi and I approached. "Hey Snapps, this is my girl Akeisha."

Akeisha grabbed my hand and shook it like I was a celebrity. I remembered her from a few of my classes years back, but I never really said anything to her. I pulled my hand back and introduced Lexi, she did a lazy wave. "Can we eat, I'm hungry." Lexi said as she invited herself to Akeisha's car. I shook my head and we all jumped into the little four door car and headed to *Pizza Hut*.

Lexi jumped out of the car before Akeisha could even cut it off. She walked in and started ordering. I held the door open for Rose and Akeisha then I followed them in. "Get what y'all want, I'm buying." I volunteered and they both smiled like I had just offered them something expensive.

Lexi turned from the cashier, "you buying mine too pretty boy?"

"Nigga you got money."

Lexi laughed and turned back around. I knew she was going to fuck with me about this later. After ordering, we all found a booth to sit in. We sat around laughing and talking and then an older lady walked over to our table stopping our conversation.

"Mom…" Rose said.

"Don't mom me. Y'all have permission to be off campus?"

"Mom we're seniors we get to leave for lunch."

"It better just be lunch and not skipping."

Lexi and I laughed our breath.

"Who are these two?"

"I'm Sasha." I gave my real name so she wouldn't clown me.

"And I'm Lexi."

Rose's mom looked over at Rose then back at us and I was sure it was because we were two girls dressed like boys sitting with her straight daughters. I knew exactly what suspicion was going on in her mind. "Shouldn't you be at work?" Rose asked mom.

"I'm on lunch." Rose's mom smiled. "You kids enjoy your lunch and get back to class." She said lowering her head and under-eyeing us all before she walked off to grab her order.

We all continued to chat until our food came then we ate and headed back to school to finished our first day. I was ready to see where this friendship was going to go.

Rose

I made it through my first day of school and I had only cried once. I was proud of myself as I lay in my bed looking over my list for the things I was going to need for the first semester. I still felt sick on the inside, but at least it wasn't showing on my face. My cell phone interrupted my thoughts. I picked up.

"Hello."

"Trick why didn't you tell me it was Snapps that we were having lunch with today?"

"…Because I didn't want you acting like a fangirl. I knew if you were caught off guard you'd be too nervous to embarrass yourself."

"I don't like you at all right now."

I laughed, "you'll get over it."

"Eventually, but still." Akeisha paused. "I swear that girl gets finer every year."

"How is it possible that you've had a crush on the same girl for five years?"

"I don't know I just have to have her."

"Well, get her, because I'm tired of hearing about it." I laughed again.

"The same way I had to hear about the crush you had on Emmitt before he finally talked to you."

"I don't want to talk about Emmitt," I stood from my bed to go into the kitchen and the phone beeped in my ear. "Hold on. Girl this is Snapps let me see what she wants." I clicked over.

"Hello"

"Hey you busy?"

"Not really what's up?"

"I just wanted to check on you make sure you weren't hiding in your bathroom crying or anything."

"Haha, no I'm actually about to eat cereal."

"At 8:30 at night?"

"That's the best time."

"So I was thinking we should do something this week."

"Like what?"

"A movie or something; I figured I could at least keep you busy until you get over ole boy."

"Aren't you sweet, I'd like that."

"Cool, I'll let you get to your cereal then."

"Ok later." We hung up and I clicked back over. "Kei, you still there?"

"I was about to hang up. What did she want?"

"Just to hang out…"

"Oh okay."

"What?"

"Nothing…"

"You're lying. You only say oh okay when you feel some type of way."

"That is not true."

"Okay whatever you say. I'm about to eat my cereal and go to bed. I'll see you in the morning." I hung up the phone and prepared my cereal.

CHAPTER 2

Snapps

"Okay so what do you want to see?" I asked Rose.

"Hmm Sparkle, oh no! The Campaign! Wait…Step Up 4."

"Girl pick one. We can come back and see the other two."

"Alright then I'll go with something funny and say the Campaign."

I walked up to the window. "Two for the Campaign," I spoke into the speaker on the glass then slid twenty dollars to the cashier. She handed me our tickets and we walked in.

"So if you paid for my ticket is this like, a date?" Rose asked.

I started to stutter, "Uh …n-n-no…its…its…not a date."

"Rose laughed, "I'm just messing with you, thanks for getting my ticket." Rose smiled.

"Yeah, cool, no problem." I said stuffing my hands into my pockets and walking behind her. "You want popcorn or something?"

"Yeah and a Coke Icee."

I purchased our snacks then we walked to find our screen. Rose wanted to sit all the way at the top so she could throw popcorn at the people below. This was the first time I was at the movies with a girl and it wasn't a date. I didn't know how to feel sitting beside Rose and I couldn't put my arm around her. I watched her from the corner of my eye most of the movie. She laughed, she tossed popcorn, she sipped her drink, and she basically sat beside me with ease just enjoying herself.

After the movie ended we headed out, but I wasn't ready to bring her home. "You hungry?"

"A little."

"What do you have a taste for?"

"Ooooh she looked around outside and spotted Friday's on the same street as the movie theater. "Let's go there."

"Okay let's go." I said then we headed to my car.

"Let's walk over there. It's not that far." Rose suggested.

"I'm fine with that."

We walked over to the restaurant and were seated immediately since it was a weekday and there wasn't a large crowd. I sat across from Rose and stared at her from behind my menu.

The waitress took our drink orders and we ordered flatbread for an appetizer.

"How come I've never met you before?" I asked Rose.

"I don't know."

"I've never even heard of you."

22

"I've heard of you."

"How?"

"My friend Akeisha."

"Yeah, I've had quite a few classes with Akeisha."

Rose laughed.

"What?"

"Nothing…"

"Uh huh…"

"Really it's nothing. I promised to never tell you."

"Saying that just makes me more curious."

"You'll just have to be curious."

"Fine, new subject then," I rested my hands in my lap, "is it just you and your mom?"

"Yeah…"

"Where's your dad, if I can ask that."

"We don't know. He was in the military and he went missing."

"Damn that's messed up."

"Yeah, my mom was messed up about it for a while. She said he only got to hold me once when I was born then he was deployed and never came back."

"Were they married?"

"No..."

"Okay we don't have to talk about this." I said to her as disturbing memories of my own father attempted to rush into my brain. It wasn't the time or the place for a conversation that deep or serious.

The waitress brought out appetizers and took our Entrée order. We sat and chit chatted about more things in our lives just to get to know each other. I

23

learned all the basics like her favorite color, favorite number, favorite food, and all that jazz. Rose was truly beautiful inside and out and learning things about her only made me want her more.

She enjoyed my company so much that she pulled out her phone and marked dates on the calendar on it for us to hang out. I told her I would keep her busy and I planned on sticking to that promise. Her ex-boyfriend wouldn't exist in any part of her mind when I was done with her.

Rose

My phone had been going off all night. Emmitt would not stop calling and in-between that Akeisha was texting for a play by play of my hang-out session with Snapps. I just wanted to tell Snapps so badly that Akeisha liked her, but I dare not break my promise not to tell. I wasn't even sure at how to hint at telling Snapps Akeisha wanted her.

For a long time I couldn't understand Akeisha's obsession with this girl, but after spending time with her I understood why. Snapps was too sweet for her own good, sort of weak in a sense to me though. I thought it was about time I made a new friend. I found it funny that the first new friend I decided to make was also gay and the crush of my best friend. I was surrounded by the rainbow. I laughed at my own thought.

"Going crazy over there?" Snapps asked.
"No just thinking about something."
"Oh…"

The waitress brought us our food and killed the awkwardness that was about to approach with my random laughed. I exhaled relieved and picked up my silverware. I was ready to stuff my face and enjoy my meal.

There was more interesting conversation between chews, but we kept it light since we were still getting the feel of each other as people. Snapps was easy to talk to. I had no idea what Akeisha was so intimidated. I'd get them together the best I could.

Snapps

Rose and I ate until we were stuffed. I paid the bill then we headed back to her house. I didn't want her mom to cuss me out for bringing her in late on a school night. That was the who reason for picking a five o'clock movie.

It was 8:40 on the dot when I pulled up in front of Rose's door. Her mother was getting ready to leave. She pulled up beside my car after she backed out of the driveway. I rolled down my window when she stopped. "Sasha right?" She said.

"Yes ma'am."

"I guess I'm going to be seeing you around often?"

"As often as your Rose wants to be bothered I guess. "I laughed.

"Uh huh, y'all better not be up to nothing y'all don't have no business."

"Mom!" Rose yelled from the passenger seat and gave her mother a look..

25

"Just kidding with you guys. I have a date Rose I'll see you in the morning."

"Okay."

"Goodnight Sasha." Rose's mother said then rolled up her window and pulled off.

Rose shook her head, "that lady has issues."

"All moms have issues."

"That's true." Rose smiled. "Well, Snapps I have to say I really enjoyed myself."

"Good, that was the purpose of this mission."

"We're still on for our other two movies this week right?"

"Yep, and downtown and the mall next week."

"Are you always this good of a friend?"

"I try to be." I smiled.

"Keep it up and I just might let you stick around." Rose smiled.

"What? Girl you better hope you stick around."

"Whatever." Rose laughed and popped my arm then hopped out of my car and waved goodbye.

I waved back then pulled off thinking *one step at a time.*

CHAPTER 3

Rose

I sat in my bed looking at old photos of
Emmitt and me still trying to find the strength to rip
them up. It was still hard for me to deal with the fact
that it was so easy for him to walk away from us like
we never happened. I sat wondering if Emmitt even
missed me at all. Did boys sit around looking at old
pictures and listening to sad songs like girls did? I
slammed the book shut and rolled over on my back,
watching as my ceiling fan spun around and around.
Getting over him wouldn't be so hard if memories
didn't haunt me. He was my first, how was I
supposed to forget that?

I closed my eyes remembering the first time I
let him into me. I touched my face lightly, pretending
it was his hand that was about to run across my skin. I
moved my hand down my neck and to my chest as I
remembered how gentle he was as he held me
beneath his muscular body. He kissed me a thousand
times, kissed me until my breathing was steady and
my heart was calmed. I asked him if it would hurt and

he promised me that it wouldn't. I moved my hands down between my legs remembering the pressure I felt as he pushed his was through my innocence. I squeezed my eyes shut tightly and he told me to open them. He wanted to see my green eyes. I remembered wondering if I sounded like a porn star as I moaned into his ear and dug my nails into his back. He went slowly the whole time and then he pulled out when he came. I never made him use condoms. I trusted him so much. How could he...

"Rose!" My mother yelled from downstairs and I snapped from my misery. I jumped up from my bed and ran to my door to see what she wanted.

"Yes," I yelled back.

"Emmitt is on the line for you."

A puzzled look appeared on my face. I wondered if he could feel me thinking about him. I stood and placed my hand on my head unsure of what to do or what to say. I didn't want to look too desperate like I was sitting around waiting for an apology. He had started this game and I was going to finish it, "tell him I'm busy!" I yelled downstairs to my mother.

"You sure?" my mother yelled back.

"Yes, tell him I'm *busy*!"

My mother did as I told her to. I walked back into my room and shut my door and I could hear her feet coming up the steps. She walked into my room. "You okay?"

"Yeah, I think so."

"Why didn't you take the call?"

"What was I supposed to say mom?"

28

"Anything or nothing, maybe he would have done all the talking."

"There was nothing he could have said to make me feel better."

"You don't know that sweetie; maybe something in his words would have provided closure for you. You're too young to be bitter."

"I'm not bitter."

"You're also too young to think you know it all."

I laughed at my mother as she pulled my door shut then pushed it back open again. "You need to sleep out tonight. I'm having company."

"Aw mom do I have to?"

"You know the routine."

"You've been doing this for years. I don't think you're boyfriends care about meeting me or if I'm home or not.

"I care…"

"Fine, I'll call my new friend Snapps. I'm sure she'd love my company."

"Snapps? "

"Sasha…"

"The gay girl I keep seeing you with?" she raised her eyebrow.

"Mom what does her being gay have to do with anything?"

"I don't know you tell me. You get your heart broken and the first thing you do is start hanging with a lesbian. Don't let one man make you change how you feel about everything."

"You're kidding right? You don't think I'm gay do you?"

"I'm just making a statement."

"No you're accusing me and if I was gay it wouldn't be because I was influenced. You do know that Akeisha is gay right?"

"Uh huh I know it, but she's not that attractive, so I don't expect you to swoon over her, but that Snapps…"

"Maybe you're the gay one mom since your hinting at how attractive Snapps is." I said joking to my mother. I had to agree that Snapps was attractive. It wasn't hard to tell why the gay girls at school were dying to be with her and the straight ones wanted her to turn them out. Akeisha practically in love and for years I never knew who Snapps was and why bitches went crazy, but now see why and getting to know her helps me know why.

"I can say when someone is attractive that won't make me gay. I'm a very secure woman. You on the other hand are young and impressionable."

"Mom get out of my room."

"I'm just saying, you've known her a couple weeks and you're doing a sleepover already. I know about that lesbian U-Haul stuff."

I fell out laughing since I didn't even know what that meant, but had a pretty good idea. Mu mom walked out and closed the door behind her laughing as she walked away.

Snapps

I sat in my bed with my ear buds in my ear, bobbing my head to the new *Drake* album, while I scrolled through other music on my iPod. I felt my cell phone vibrate on my bed under my leg. I picked it up and Rose's name flashed across the screen. I smiled and pulled the ear buds from my ears and picked up. "What's up love?"

"What are you doing?"

"Chillin'"

"I hate when people say that, what the hell is chillin'?"

"I'm listening to music girl." I laughed and she returned the chuckle.

"You think I could sleep by you tonight?"

"Yeah, why what's up?"

"My mom is having her man friend over and she wants the house to herself."

"Oh cool, so you chose me over your best friend?"

"Shut up. I love Akeisha, but her house is always dirty and it's hard for me to sleep in clutter."

"Okay, well, what time you coming?"

"Around seven, Akeisha is going to drop me off."

"Alright." I said then we hung up. I hopped out of bed and started cleaning my room or she wouldn't be able to sleep in here either. I knocked over the pictures sitting on my nightstand and my mother swung my door open. "What is all that noise you making in here girl?"

"I'm cleaning up."

"Cleaning up? Who coming to my house?"

"Rose…"

"Mmm I should have known."

"She sleeping over is that okay?"

31

"I guess it is, but you better leave this door open."

"Mom she's straight."

"Yeah so was I in 1987 then Ashley happened and I was bisexual then lesbian and now I'm straight again." she side-eyed me. "That girl might use you as an experiment; better watch yourself with this new breed of lil chicken heads."

"Nobody says chicken head anymore."

"I do." she said walking out of my room and closing the door.

I continued to clean up picking up all my clothes from the floor and straightening my bed. I walked past the full length mirror in my room and checked myself then smiled. I was a pretty nigga. I rubbed my hands across my face turning from side to side swinging my dreads and admiring my dimples. I laughed thinking to myself that light skinned dudes might be played out, but light-skinned studs were always going to be in.

Rose pulled up a little bit before seven. My mother answered the door and gave her an ugly glare as she walked by. I tried to keep calm. Although I knew that Rose wasn't into girls I still wanted her and I felt kind of guilty sometimes being her friend because I knew my intentions but I also knew the possibility of it never happening.

Rose walked into my bedroom and sat on the edge of my bed to remove her shoes. She placed them neatly near my bed and sat her overnight bag to the side. She walked around checking out my room. "Can I ask you a question?"

"Yeah…"

"Why does this room look like a boy's room?" she laughed.

"I'm a boy Damon," I joked as I quoted one of my favorite lines from *Next Friday*.

"No, but seriously explain this whole gay thing to me again with the girls who dress like boys."

"You mean studs."

"Oh so you call yourselves studs?"

"AG's, doms, whatever…I told you that."

"I forgot," she tapped her chin "okay, so, if I were gay what would I be since I don't dress like you?"

"A femme"

"You gays are serious with the labels. I can't keep up." she laughed.

"You gays?"

"What was I supposed to say?"

I smiled. "Nothing it's just funny that you have a gay best friend and you know nothing about gay people."

"Me and Akeisha don't talk about that kind of stuff. I mean we talk about our relationship problems and you, but all that other crap is just too technical." she flopped back down on my bed.

"Why you always talking about me with that girl?" I scrunched my face and Rose laughed. "How long have you and Akeisha been friends?" I said sitting on the opposite side of the bed.

"Since the seventh grade, but don't change the subject, why do you even like girls?"

"I was born this way."

"Bullshit, no one is born liking the same sex."

"Can you prove that theory?"

33

"No…"

"Exactly"

"So you have never had a boyfriend?"

"Nope and don't want one."

"But how can you knock something you haven't tried?"

"My legs in the air while a nigga ramming me? No thanks ma I'll pass."

Rose laughed hard. "It's nothing like that."

"It's exactly like that no matter how you say it."

"It actually feels kind of good."

"You aren't really about to sit here and tell me dick stories are you?"

"Would you rather hear vagina stories?"

"If you have some," I smiled.

She picked up my pillow and hit me hard with it. "Okay better question, why don't you have a girlfriend?"

"I'm picky."

"Nobody is that picky."

"I am. I've dated two chicks my whole life. The one in middle school who showed me the game and my most recent ex who is much older than me and fucked over me for her ex and used me for my allowance."

Rose laughed. "I'm sorry I'm laughing, but I didn't expect the allowance part." she wiped away her smile, "I'm sorry about what your ex did."

"It's all good, so are you going to survey me all night or are you going to shower so we can get some sleep for school?"

"I showered at home." she smiled then stood to get her bag from the corner. She pulled her clothes off right there in front of me and changed. This was going to be a hard friendship to be a part of. "I have another question." Rose asked as she pulled up her night pants.

"What now?"

"What is u-hauling?"

I fell back on my bed and laughed to tears. "Where did you hear that?"

"My mom said it."

"I think your mom and my mom have been talking on the phone."

I laughed a bit more at Rose's questions, which were the typical ones that were asked by straight girls, but I answered them. Rose and I sat up half the night talking as if we didn't have school the next day. She continued to grill me about the gay community and I continued to tell her why I'd always be a part of it. I was starting to think that even attempting to get at her would be pointless since she was trying to convince me why dick was so good. I wanted to gag and puke the more she told me about her sex life with college boy. The only good thing was that he had been her only partner, so she had not been marked a hoe. I let Rose talk until she dozed off then I pulled the cover up over her body and slowly drifted right behind her.

CHAPTER 4

Akeisha

I walked to my car frustrated because I had called Rose several times. She was the one who told me to call and wake her up and she wasn't even answering the phone. If she didn't pick up this one last time I was going to school without her and she could walk. I dialed once more.

"Hello," She answered laughing loudly in my ear.

"Damn bitch what were you doing? I called you like ten times."

"I know I'm so sorry. I was eating breakfast with Snapps and her mom, that lady is a trip."

"Okay that's all fine and well, but you could have at least texted me. I got out of bed all early to wake your high yellow ass up."

"I'm sorry Kei." Rose pouted.

"Well, I'm about to be on my way to get you."

"Oh no it's okay, Snapps has a car. I'll ride with her. I'll catch you at lunch." She said then hung up.

That short sentence showed me just how much we hadn't been talking. I didn't even know Snapps had a car. She always rode around with her friend Lexi. I guess she was pulling out the wheels for Rose today. I looked at the phone pissed and tossed it on the passenger seat. Rose had been brushing me off for the last couple of weeks for Snapps and I didn't appreciate it. Every time we talked it was Snapps and I are doing this and Snapps and I are doing that. They hung out downtown at music stores, and they had gone to the movies three times just last week. I thought Rose would have at least invited me along since she knew I liked Snapps. I started to feel some type of way about having to share my best friend with my crush. I walked outside and got into my car and rode to school with my music blasting to help keep me calm and distracted.

I pulled into the student parking lot and waited by Rose's first class and of course she walked up with Snapps. I smiled as they approached just to keep my aggravation from showing. "Can I talk to you?" I asked Rose.

"Yeah, of course." she said as she stood beside Snapps.

"Alone? No offense Snapps."

"None taken Shorty." Snapps said.

I pulled Rose off to the side. "What you too good to ride in my lil beat up *Honda* now?"

"What are you talking about?"

"You've been tossing me to the side for awhile, are you gay now or something?"

"No! Snapps is just cool."

"Yeah, but I'm your best friend, you don't even come over anymore, what was that all about last night sleeping over by her and not me?"

38

"She asked me to."

"Yeah okay." I said rolling my eyes.

"I'm mad you getting all in your feelings about this. It's only been a few weeks Kei, you're still my best friend." she said with conviction then leaned back and looked me up and down, "Ah, wait, I wonder if it has something to do with the crush you have on you Snapps."

"You didn't tell her did you?!"

"Of course not, I can keep a secret, but if you don't say something eventually I will. You have to learn to be more aggressive mama or you'll never get what you want and Snapps is a cutie, you better grab her quick before someone else does."

I felt as though she was saying to me before *she* does, but I refused to believe that, so I just simply said, "Put in a good word for me." in hopes that she actually would.

"You know I got you, we're going to the mall later, and you should come."

The anger started to fade. "Cool, I'll meet y'all there." I gave Rose a partial smile.

"Alright Kei." Rose hugged me then we went our separate ways for class.

I calmed down after talking to Rose since her being Snapps' friend was a good way for me to get close to Snapps too. I couldn't wait to hang out in the mall with her. I had liked Snapps for years, but she always had a girlfriend, well up until this year. I wanted to give her some time to get over her ex, everybody had heard about their breakup and the fist fight in the parking lot between Snapps the ex-girlfriend's ex that got Snapps suspended and the ex

39

arrested for coming onto the school property. I didn't want to crowd her, but she was clearly doing okay from what I was seeing from her friendship with Rose.

At fifth period the bell rang for lunch and I saw them sitting in the cafeteria. I walked over to join them. They were talking and laughing. "Hey," I said then took a seat.

"Hey Kei," Snapps said as she did a head nod and I tried not to blush too hard. Rose smiled at me and we all started talking until this boy named Greg that had been crushing on Rose for years walked over to the table.

"What's up Rose." he said and smiled.

"Hey Greg." Rose looked up.

"I heard about what Emmitt did. I hope you're doing okay though."

I rolled my eyes thinking that he was pathetic, but Rose ate that type of attention up. She loved the boys that fell at her feet and clung to her every word as if she was a goddess. She knew in the back of her mind that she'd never give them the time of day except to use them and they knew it too, but they'd rather be used than invisible to her.

"I'm making it. I have great friends to keep me distracted." she said as she rubbed her hand over Snapps shoulder and Snapps placed her hand around her waist for reassurance that she indeed had a good "friend". It made me uncomfortable to see them touching that way and I tried hard not to let it show on my face, but I knew Rose would notice so I pretended to have a text from my mom. "I gotta step out to call my mom y'all." I stood from the table and walked away to gather myself holding my phone up to my ear pretending to talk to the nobody on the other end. I adjusted my expression, inhaled and exhaled, and then walked back over to the table.

"Everything okay?" Rose asked.

"Yeah she just needs me to come right home after school."

"Aw man you can't come to the mall with us?" She pouted, but I had the feeling she wasn't that upset or maybe it was just my own mind playing tricks on me.

"Nah she needs me to do something, I'll just catch up with you guys later." I said then stood again. "I have to get my books for my next class from my car, just call me tonight or something." I walked off.

I couldn't admit to myself that I was jealous of my best friend and I wouldn't admit it so I'd just avoid it for as long as I could. I knew that she would never go behind my back and flirt with someone that she knew I liked, shit Rose wasn't even gay. It was just me being insecure and I had to shake it off. There had been plenty of times that the person I liked went for Rose, but she never went for them, so I had to tell myself that Rose would come through for me no matter what I thought I was feeling. I walked away to shake the ill emotions. I'd get Snapps. I had been waiting too long not to.

Rose

Snapps and I stood out front after school waiting on her best friend Lexi to pull up from around back, so we could all head to the mall. I wanted Snapps to just take her car, but she argued that it made no sense when we were all going to the same place anyway. Lexi rolled up with her music blasting and all of her windows down. Snapps hopped in the front and I slid into the back. Lexi pulled off quickly and pulled a blunt from her middle console.

"Damn bitch you couldn't at least wait until we were a few blocks away from school?" Snapps yelled over the music and leaned her seat back.

"I waited eight hours, I'm lighting this shit." Lexi laughed.

"You need to leave that shit alone."

"For what? I ain't pissing for nobody's test or team no time soon."

Snapps shook her head as Lexi blew smoke and I sat in the back bobbing my head to whatever song was on the radio. "Is this a girl?" I yelled.

"Yeah"

"What's her name?"

"Huh?"

"What's her name?"

"*Shaky Shawn*"

"I've never heard of her."

"Because she's a stud rapper, niggas don't take us seriously. There are quite a few that go hard."

"What's the name of this song? I need to download it."

"*Full time hustla*, look her up on YouTube, ShakyShawnTv."

"Cool, thanks," I said and continued to listen to the song and ride. Lexi was a terrible driver. She sped through lights and slung around corners. I was so scared for my life that I buckled my seatbelt in the backseat. She turned her music down when we came to another red light. "So redbone you not worried people will think you're gay walking around with pretty boy over here?"

"Not for real. I really don't care."

"I heard that," She snickered then choked a little on smoke and turned her music back up. We pulled up to the mall and I had never been happier about placing my feet on solid ground. "I'll catch y'all in a minute; I'm going meet this lil freak in the food court." Snapps threw up two fingers and we walked in through the opposite entrance. Snapps opened the door for me and I stepped in.

"What you came to get out of here anyway?" I asked.

"I need some new shoes."

"Girl you just brought shoes last week."

"I know that, get out of my business."

Snapps and I walked down to *Footlocker* so she could look at the shoes she wanted. I sat and waited. I had never really worn anything other than heels or sandals so I didn't even know how to shop for tennis outside of the black or brown ones we were allowed to wear to school. Snapps pulled a display shoe from the wall and an associate walked over to get her size. She came and sat down beside me with the display shoe in her hand. "You like this shoe?"

"It's cute I guess."

"You guess?" She shook her head. "You want some?"

"Tennis?"

"Yeah girl, I'm tired of seeing you in heels and shit, relax sometimes."

"I can relax in flats."

"What size shoe do you wear?"

"I'm not telling you."

"If you don't I'll just make them measure it." Loud laughter from behind interrupted our conversation and made us both turn around. Snapps turned back fast the instant she looked over her shoulder.

"What?" I asked puzzled.

"That's my ex and her bitch."

"So…"

"So I still want to beat the snot out of her when I see her."

"For what? You're over her right?"

"Been…"She said as she looked back again.

"Okay then…"

"Shit!"

"What?"

"She's bringing her stupid ass over here."

I eased closer to Snapps, sliding my arm behind her back. If I wasn't good at anything else I was a pro at making bitches jealous. I removed my right shoe to reveal my red painted toe nails and eased my leg across Snapps' lap as her ex walked over. "Baby I need a sock so I can try on the shoes you're getting me." I said loud enough for her ex to hear. There was nothing worse than seeing your ex happy and doing better with someone who looked better

44

than you. Her old bitch was cute and definitely a looker when she turned around because that ass was fat, but she still didn't have shit on me and I didn't even like bitches.

Snapps caught on and reached for a free sock from the container near us, pulling it over my foot. Her ex moved closer. She looked as though she wanted to come say something, but she kept her distance and I became more touchy-feely with Snapps, running my finger across her face and kissing her neck every time I felt her looking. Snapps smiled and blushed. Snapps' ex and her girl paid for their shoes and as she walked by I laughed. "Bitch," I said and dared her to turn around. She took on my dare and stopped dead in her tracks.

"Beg u pardon." She said swinging her store bought hair behind her.

"You heard me."

She moved toward me and her girlfriend grabbed her arm. "Let it go."

"Yeah let it go." I smiled.

"Miseh u lucky seh we dehinna public and mi nuhwaah police come fi mi, but watch mi an u yuhlata."

Her accent threw me a little, but the words lucky, police, and later gave me a pretty good idea of what she had said, "I wouldn't bet on it. I don't hang around where trash piles up." I laughed and swung the hair I had grown for seventeen years.

Snapps' ex dropped her bag and charged at me, but Snapps stood in her way. "Get the fuck on with all that Anya."

"Yuh bitch start it."

45

"Just like your bitch came up to my school to start shit with me and got her ass handed to her? You want a repeat of that situation and more jail time?"

Anya backed off and picked up her bags. Her scary ass girlfriend just stood there waiting for everything to go down. Snapps must have really beaten that girl to sleep the way she kept her distance. She didn't even check her for handling her girl. She just grabbed her hand and they walked out of the store. Snapps shook her head and sat back down laughing. "You are something else. You are too pretty to be acting hood," Snapps said.

"I've been around Akeisha too long."

"It's kind of hot though."

"You would think so and by-the-way I wear an eight," I smiled and put my foot in Snapps face and she pushed it away still laughing at what happened. "You never told me that you're ex was Jamaican."

"My bad"

"I barely understood a word she said."

"I was with her for two years and couldn't understand her." We both laughed again.

"I hear women from any island are crazy."

"Believe everything you've heard," Snapps shook her head and I changed the subject.

"So what did you think about that guy Greg that came to the table today?"

"He cool"

"He's liked me since forever; I think I want to go on a date with him."

"If that takes your mind off ole boy then I'm with it."

46

"I'm not even worried about Emmitt anymore. He called my house the other day and I told my mom to tell him I was busy. That's my excuse until I find a new one." I paused. "You know, he blew my phone up the whole time we were on our friendship date the first night?"

"Word?"

"Yep, and I didn't feel the need to answer."

"Well you're making progress."

"Speaking of dates though, how would you feel about a double date?"

"With who?"

"Me silly and you and Akei…" Snapps cut me off before I could finish.

"Heeeellll no"

"Why not?!"

"Look at her and look at me."

"Akeisha is not that bad looking."

"I'll just say she really isn't my type to avoid sounding mean."

I slapped Snapps on the arm, "Stop it."

"I don't have anything against big girls because I have crossed some in my day that I would toss, but Akeisha man I don't know."

"Just go on one date for me, please."

"Man, what I get?"

"What do you want?"

"You gotta twist my dreads and come clean my room for a week."

"Done"

"Since it's that easy…"

"Don't push it." I said as the associate brought out Snapps' shoes. Now maybe Akeisha would start

47

to feel better about me hanging with Snapps since I did what I was asked to do.

CHAPTER 5

Akeisha

I helped my mother as she set up outside for the barbeque. I was anxious because Rose had invited Snapps to be my date and she was bringing Greg as hers. This would be the first time that I'd get a chance to really impress Snapps and show her I'd be better to her and for her than all the other skanks she had chosen to be with.

I paced back and forth forgetting what it was that I was supposed to be doing as I thought of the possibilities of tonight. My mother kept calling my name each time I spaced out, but her voice was a whisper to me because my main focus was Snapps. I still remembered the first time I saw her. It was our seventh grade year. She walked into the cafeteria in all her glory with her peach-yellow skin from her black mother and white father that I'm sure was salted perfectly for my tongue to run across. She was dressed half way feminine with a tight, black and white *American Eagle* t-shirt on and denim fitted jeans and *Sperry's* to complete the outfit. Two shiny diamonds sat in her ears and she wore a short, silver cross pendant around her neck, which has been replaced with the longer one over the years. I was sure that she was still in that "I dress this way because I'm comfortable not gay" stage. Most studs went through that stage, trying too hard to be feminine and not hard enough to be who they were. Snapps wore her hair in a flowing roller wrap before she decided to dread up like most studs these days in what I call the *Lil Wayne Era.* I would sit in the gym and watch her sit between girl's legs and get her hair braided weekly thinking *I could do that.* I was way beyond having it bad for Ms. Sasha "Snapps" Adams.

I remember watching the way that she walked. I knew she was gay even if she didn't know it yet and. I wanted to be her first. I wanted to sink my teeth into her, but Kelsey Conway had gotten to her first and I hated her for it as they walked up the halls together, placing their books in each other's lockers, and passing notes in class for two and a half long years. I had written Snapps so many unsent letters, just to get the thoughts of her out of my head. I had to accept that I was the defeated girl since I didn't have the courage enough to open my mouth and get to her first. She belonged to someone else.

The letters never really helped, because something would happen every day that gave me something else to admire. Rose used to tease me and tell me I was obsessed. She never found Snapps all that attractive, which I was sure, was because she refused to believe anyone could be more beautiful than she was. She kept her distance from Snapps and for years they had never shared as much as a classroom and since Snapps was always occupied with a girlfriend she never noticed Rose. Part of me was happy that they had never known each other, because in my heart I knew Snapps would go for Rose over me and although Rose wasn't gay I always felt like she'd date her just to prove the point that Snapps wasn't really worth admiring.

"Akeisha...Akeisha!" My mother called out for my attention.

"Huh?" I snapped out of yet another trance.

"Go get the door girl."

I walked to the door and opened it. Several people walked in at once. I hugged a few of my cousins and kissed the cheeks of my aunts. I followed behind them to the back yard and help them place the dishes that they volunteered to bring. I walked in and out of the house checking the time. I started to wonder if Rose and Snapps were going to show up.

Two hours had passed and the doorbell finally rang. I walked and opened the door and my heart dropped as I laid eyes on Snapps. Her dreads hung down past her shoulders and she had a fitted cap pulled down over them. I loved when she wore her hair like that. "Come on in." I moved to the side, "everyone is in the backyard. There are some extra chairs in the kitchen."

"You want me to just bring them all out?" Snapps asked.

I smiled, "yeah I'd appreciate it." Snapps headed for the kitchen and Rose and Greg walked in hand-in-hand. I was never happier to see Greg than I was at that very moment. As long as Greg was there Snapps and Rose couldn't make me feel like a third

51

wheel to their newly developed friendship and I could make my move on Snapps. "Cute shoes chick." I said as Rose walked by. "I'm surprised to see you in sneakers."

"Snapps bought them and insisted I wear them. I feel funny," Rose laughed.

I gritted my teeth to hide my irritation. Now they were so close that she was buying her shoe? I let the thoughts that wanted to play around in my mind fly away as I shut the door behind Rose and Greg. "Is there anything I can help with?" Greg asked.

"If you want to help Snapps set up chairs for you guys you can."

"Cool," Greg kissed Rose on the cheek and walked away. Greg was tall and skinny; not exactly the kind of guy Rose went for. His eyes were big and his lips could cool three cans of soup at a time with a single blow. If his looks weren't goofy enough the way he dressed with his skinny jeans and tight shirts added to his lameness.

"So what made you decide to finally give Greg a chance?"

"I needed a distraction. Emmitt called again and he won't stop calling."

"What did he want?"

"I don't know I keep giving my mom excuses to give him."

"Not too long ago you were hell bent on being with him and crying your eyes out constantly and now you won't even answer his call?"

"He played me Kei. I think I'll let him sweat a little longer and since him and Greg were friends someone is bound to tell him what's up," She smirked.

"You conniving trick," I pulled her and wrapped my arm around her shoulder to pull her to the backyard. Snapps and Greg were already seated and probably talking about Rose and I. We walked over to where they sat and they fell silent, which hinted to me that they were indeed talking about us. "What y'all over here talking about?" I asked.

"Nothing." Snapps said. "When can we eat?"

"Oh you're hungry now? I'll fix you a plate," I smiled.

"I can do it myself."

"No boo you relax, this is my party. I'll cater to you. You want a drink too?"

Snapps rubbed her hands up and down her jeans, "Uh, yeah, sure."

I pulled Rose, "Come on girl make your man a plate."

Rose and I fixed plates for Greg and Snapps and brought it over to them. I pulled one of the chairs close to Snapps and sat down beside her, handing her her food. I was ready to play the get to know you game. I looked over at Rose and she motioned for me to say something. "Snapps I'm really glad you came." I said to spark conversation.

"No problem ma," She dug into her food.

I couldn't think of anything else to say. "So, how's the food?"

"It's really good, your moms got skills."

"Actually I cooked. She just worked the grill."

"Word?"

"Yeah," I laughed. I loved the way she spoke. I let her finish her food then I took her plate and threw it in the trash. I offered her more, but she was full. My palms were starting to sweat as my nerves got the best of me.

"You and Kei should go take a walk." Rose said out loud.

I smiled, "you want to take a walk with me?"

Snapps looked over at Greg and Rose then she stood up. "Yeah, I guess that's cool."

I stood up and grabbed her hand, hoping she wouldn't reject me and she didn't. I turned and gave Rose the biggest smile as we walked away.

There was silence for a while as we walked. Then I spoke up, "Rose told me that you're ready to start dating again."

"Oh she did huh?" Snapps said.

I watched her facial expression, getting that feeling of rejection again, but hoping I was wrong. I had to say something quickly, anything to kill the long pause of silence. "Yeah and I mean if it's cool I was thinking we could chill sometime."

"You cool and all Akeisha, but I'm really not ready. I guess Rose didn't tell you we ran into my ex and it kind of started some drama."

Rose had told me about the mall incident and the ex, but somehow she left out the part where Snapps bought her some shoes, but I was hoping that Snapps would at least take my offer to chill, but then again in the lesbian community "dating" or "chillin" was the same thing as a relationship. I could respect her being cautious. I'd give her more time.

We walked back to my house and everyone was finally gone. Rose and Greg stayed behind and helped to clean up. Snapps and I started to help to. We pulled all the trash to the front then I hugged Greg and Rose goodbye saving Snapps last. I hugged her tight and tried to kiss her, but she turned her face and I caught her cheek. It was cool though. She just needed time. I waved goodbye to them as they pulled away.

Rose

Greg dropped Snapps off first then me. I kissed him goodbye and headed inside. The instant I closed the door behind me my mother yelled downstairs to me. "Emmitt called again."

I sighed, "What did he want?"

"I don't know Rose just call the boy please."

"Alright," I said as I headed upstairs to my room. I flopped down on my bed and held my cell phone in my hand just staring at the black screen. It was about time I just talked to him. I had deleted his number from my phone, which served no purpose since it was embedded inside my brain. I unlocked my screen and pulled up my keypad to dial his number. I hit the little green call symbol and took a deep breath.

The phone rang four times then I motioned to hang up until his deep voice vibrated through the phone. "Rose?"

I moved the phone back up to my ear, "yeah, what's up?" I paused. "Why do you keep calling?"

"I just wanted to check on you?"

"Check on me?"

"Yeah see how you were doing."

"My boyfriend of three years broke up with me, but I'm dealing."

"Rose would you stop it."

"Stop? How? You break-up with me and then keep calling as if nothing has happened. I'm hurting Emmitt."

"It will get better, just give it time."

"It's really sad how you can say that with so much ease like you never cared at all."

"I did care. I've just grown up." "He took a breath. "From what I hear you're dealing just fine with Greg."

"Greg and I are just hanging out."

"You and me used to just *hang out* all the time."

"Wow. Okay Emmitt goodbye."

"Rose..."

I hung up the phone in Emmitt's face and bit down on my bottom lip to hold on to the tears I refused to shed for him. He was so cold. I sat my phone down and pulled the pictures of him and me from beneath my bed. I could rip them up now.

I pulled the box from beneath my bed and sat it on my mattress then I walked over to my drawer and pulled out a pair of scissors. My first thought was to rip them up, but then I thought about how cute I looked in some of them and just decided to cut Emmitt out. I sat back down on my bed and my phone lit up.

"Hey Snapps."

"Don't hey Snapps me."

"What?"

"You friend tried to kiss me."

"Was she successful?"

"No."

"Then what are you bitching at me for?"

"You get on my nerves."

"You love me." I started to cut up pictures. "So, when are you and Akeisha going out on a date alone?"

"Never."

"Why not?"

"Because I don't like her like that."

"You've never even given her a chance Snapps."

"I don't need to. I know what I like. You want me to be like you and treat her like a charity case the way you do Greg?"

I held my mouth open, "I don't know treat him like a charity case."

"No? Okay so if he was just a regular guy and there had never been and Emmitt would you have given him a chance?"

"Probably not."

"My point exactly. I don't believe in leading people on. I'm not attracted to Akeisha in no way shape form or fashion and leading her own would just ruin her for the future she could have with someone who's feeling her like that."

"Well, tell her that then."

"You tell her because it's kind of cruel the way you keep forcing her on me."

"I'm not going to do that Snapps. It'll hurt her feelings just as bad if I tell her that."

"You're a horrible friend."

"I'm a great friend. Akeisha would do the same for me."

Snapps laughed, "Oh yeah?"

"Yep…"

"Alright, I'll go on one date with Akeisha and see if she's as great as you make her out to be."

I sat all the way up in the bed, "Really?"

"Yep, give me her number I'll call her right now and set it up for tomorrow."

"Okay 555-3086."

"Bye." Snapps hung up on me.

Snapps

I dialed Akeisha's number the instant that I hung up on Rose. I was going to shut her once and for all.

"Hello." Akeisha answered.

"Sup Kei?"

"Who is this?"

"Snapps"

Her tone of voice changed. "Oh hey Snapps, what's up?"

"Are you busy tomorrow?"

"Not at all…"

"You want to have dinner with me?"

"Hell yeah. I mean yes, I would love to."

"Okay cool 6:30 good for you?"

"I'll be ready."

"Iight later." I hung up the phone.

CHAPTER 6

Rose

"Mmmm yeah right there I moaned as Greg ran his tongue across my pearl the slipped right back off my spot like he had been doing half the evening. "Move back up," I pulled his head and slid down helping with the adjustment. I was never going to come at the rate we were going.

I was really missing Emmitt right now. He really knew my body and he knew how to satisfy me. I wasn't even sure what possessed me to allow Greg between my legs. My hormones were raging and it was my only option since I had spent the most time with him. Greg leaned up before I could get his tongue back on my spot. "Can I stick it in now?" He asked with a goofy expression on his face. It was clear that he had not had many encounters with girls.

"No," go back down.

Greg didn't argue. He placed his face back between my legs and resumed licking. I was slowly losing my mojo as he accomplished nothing down below. I pulled the cover over his head and let him

lick his life away as I pulled my phone from beneath the pillow. Greg was so focused on trying to get it right that he'd never notice anything going on beyond the covers. I texted
Akeisha

I didn't bother to respond with a "k" or anything because that was dumb. Greg moved the covers from over his head and looked up at me. "Can I stick it in now?"

"No!" I pushed him off of me. "I'm not even in the mood anymore."

Greg stood up and his hard dick poked out through his boxers. "Will you at least play with it?"

I exhaled and rolled my eyes. I had to find someone new to occupy my time or at least get this guy some lessons.

Akeisha

I looked out of the window waiting on Snapps to pull up. I was still shocked that she had even called last night to ask me out after rejecting my "chill" invitation. I stepped back from the window and paced back and forth. I was so nervous. My palms were sweaty and my insides were shaking. I just wanted tonight to be perfect.

I heard tires roll slowly against the concrete outside and I knew it was her. I took a deep breath then stop my pace. I opened the door and she was heading my way. "You didn't have to come in I yelled to her then closed the door behind me and locked it. I walked to her car and jumped in on her passenger side.

"What you want to eat?" Snapps asked as I shut the car door.

"Doesn't matter…"

"Applebees good?"

"Yeah works for me."

Snapps pulled off. I tried hard not to smile from ear to ear. It was like a dream come true, having you crush of so many years finally give you a chance.

I didn't want to get ahead of myself so I tried to calm myself down and remember it was just dinner.

We pulled up to the restaurant and parked. Snapps was a complete gentle "woman" opening doors for me and pulling out my chair when we were seated.

Snapps sat down and grabbed her menu and before I could stop myself I had an outburst. "I'm really nervous."

"Why?"

"I don't know. I've just want to talk to you for so long…"

"What did you think I was going to bite you or something?"

"Nah you were always kind of occupied and I never could find my words."

"Oh…"

I had to keep the conversation going. I didn't want to bore her, but I couldn't think of a single thing to say. The only common denominator between us was Rose. "Talked to Rose today?" I asked.

"No."

"Why not? I thought you two were like BFF's"

"We're friends, but Lexi is my best friend."

"Can I make a confession?"

"Yeah sure."

"I thought you and Rose had something going on. I mean since you were buying her shoes and all."

"What's wrong with that?"

"Nothing I guess. I just know Rose better than that."

"What you mean?"

"She's just not a something for nothing type of chick. Even when she was messing with Emmitt he was always buying her things, but that wasn't until after he slept with her."

Snapps facial expression never changed. I started to think that maybe if I told her all the things I knew about Rose, it would prevent her from ever wanting her and it would increase my chance. "That was her dude at the time so it's seems cool to me." Snapps said.

"Emmitt wasn't exactly that into Rose, she just likes everyone to believe that."

Snapps had a look of curiosity on her face.

"Rose was in love with Emmitt, but he was in love with somebody else and whoever it was didn't want him anymore so he started to date Rose. She knew he was used to having sex since he was older and she didn't want to have to compete with older girls so she gave him her virginity and after he started buying her things she gave it up more and more."

Snapps didn't say a word so I continued to ramble on.

"Rose let Emmitt mess over her for a long time. She's pretty, but she dumb as hell when it comes to boys."

Our waitress came with our food and I continued to tell Snapps things about Rose. It might not have tainted the image of Rose in Snapps' mind, but it might end some of the time they spend together and leave more room for me.

Snapps

As Akeisha ran her mouth all I could think about was how badly I wanted to slap Rose. She spoke so highly of Akeisha and here she was selling her out just to keep my attention. Most of what she was saying was going in one ear and out of the other because gossip never really interested me. I really thought this was a bitch move that Akeisha was pulling.

I would never sell my dawg Lexi out for a piece of pussy. I guess studs were more like dudes when it came to friendship and relationships. This dinner probably would have gone in a different direction had she found something else to blab about.

Everything she said was throwing up red flags in my head. If a bitch can't be loyal to their friend they for damn sure can't be loyal to their partner. I tried so hard not to turn up my nose at this girl. All I could think was if I should tell Rose or not.

I voted on the not since Akeisha had years on me as far as being her friend went and if I told Rose, Akeisha would probably just twist my words. It was definitely drama I didn't need. I was going to be playing the duck and dodge game with Akeisha until she got the hint. I wouldn't even stick the head of my strap inside this girl. She was a snake and I didn't like it all and Rose had no idea.

CHAPTER 7
(Senior year)

Snapps

I spent the rest of the school year, an entire summer, and majority of my senior year avoiding Akeisha and her advances and playing third wheel to Greg and Rose. Akeisha wanted to be with me so bad, but she just wasn't my type. Every now and then I'd be nice to her because of Rose and her bribes. I was getting new shoes and my gas tank filled up. There was no way that I could say no to that with the way gas prices were raising. I really couldn't understand why she wouldn't just tell Akeisha there was no way in hell that she and I would ever be together. Instead Rose would invite her everywhere that we went and I'd have to deal with it.

The dodging was finally going to come to an end since this was our final day of class. I'd be college bound. I had gotten a full ride to four schools and now it was just a matter of choice.

Rose walked up to me with a ton of papers in her hands. "What is all that?" I asked.

"Acceptance letters!"

"Congrats love."

"Thanks! What colleges were you accepted into?"

I shook my head. "What makes you think I want to go to college?"

"You're a straight 'A' student Snapps you better go. We could go to the same college and get lost on campus together."

I liked the idea of getting lost with Rose. "Sounds like a plan. *LSU, Spellman, Alabama State, and Howard* want me."

"You fucking nerd."

"Don't hate."

"So have you thought about a date for the prom?"

"I'm going alone. I'll just follow you and Greg around all night as usual."

She laughed. "I believe you too, but what about Akeisha?"

I rolled my eyes at Rose. She just wasn't getting it. "Aww come on not this Akeisha stuff again. That girl has been pushing up on me ever since you forced me to that barbeque at her house. I've tried every way possible to tell her I'm not interested since you won't and she still tries."

"She really likes you Snapps. You have to admire her persistence."

"I really like Mac and cheese, but you don't see me in the store trying to buy it all so no one else can have any."

"Big girls need love too Snapps."

"Big girls do need love too, but that's just not up my alley, so she won't be getting it from me. I'd get Lexi high and put a dress on her before I take Akeisha anywhere."

Rose popped my arm and we fell out laughing. She tried to convince me to take her to the prom the entire day. Rose was a terrible friend because she could have told that girl better, but instead she was telling me how funny she was, how smart she was, how cool and kind she was, but all I could see in my head was her size and nothing else about her stood out that would at least make me consider her. I understood fully that books can't be judged by the cover, but I believed wholeheartedly that most connections were made through physical attraction first. I wasn't trying to be a dick, I was just being honest and Rose wasn't respecting that. I'd think to date a big girl if she was attractive, because at 6'1" I could handle one, but it wouldn't be Akeisha. I didn't like the way she dressed, the way she talked, her sneaky essence, or the way she threw herself at me. I had no desire for breast that would need both of my hands just to grab one or for sliding my fingers into a creased back. I needed more of a challenge, someone I could handle with ease. I needed Rose.

Rose

Akeisha would never forgive me if I didn't get Snapps to take her prom. My lies were finally going to catch up with me. I had been telling Akeisha for months that Snapps really liked her and just needed time to come around. I told her that Snapps talked about her all the time and I just left out the negative things. It was becoming a job protecting Akeisha's feelings when it came to this ridiculous crush that she had on Snapps. I admired her ambitious spirit, but it was clear as day that Snapps had zero interest in her. I had run out of bribes and I only had a few hours to change Snapps' mind or I'd just have to find a new lie. Maybe I could tell her that Snapps would meet her there or something, because I just couldn't tell her the truth.

I picked up my cell phone and called Snapps.

She picked up on the first ring. "Didn't I just see you at school? You better not be calling me to tell me about Akeisha. The answer is no."

"Oh come on Snapps," I begged, "you would seriously rather go alone?"

"Rose you've been selling your best friend to me since last school year. I…don't…like…her."

"Fine I give up then."

"Good, it's about damn time. Now I'm changing the subject. Did you book the rooms?"

"Yep, two suites at the Hilton."

"Iight then I'm about to head out with my mom to pick up this rental."

"Oh your *Kia* wasn't good enough?" I laughed.

"Hell no I have to ride in style for Prom girl. It's the last dance."

"I guess your right I'll see you at the dance." I hung up defeated.

Snapps

Lights flashed and music blasted as I stepped foot into the prom. I was so mad at Lexi for letting me go to the dance alone. I had even told her she could wear a tux and all she could say was that she wasn't a suit and tie type nigga. I left her be. I handed a teacher my ticket and headed on in. I searched around for Rose, but she spotted me first and it was the first day of eleventh grade year all over again as she walked up to me smiling. Her hair hung in curls around her bare shoulders. She wore a soft pink halter dress that was split up the side to show off those beautiful legs that I admired whenever she was around. "Damn," I said as she approached.

"What?" She responded to my slip of the tongue.

"You look beautiful."

"Thank you," she blushed, "you look really good yourself; you're killing most of the dudes here in a tux."

"I mean I do what I can," I smiled pretending to be more suave than I actually was. Rose hugged me and the scent of her perfume crept up my nose. I closed my eyes and let it intoxicate me. "You smell good."

Rose pulled back still smiling at me, "thank you. Well, I have to get back to Greg, save me a dance?"

"Whenever you're ready," I bit my bottom lip and watched her walk off. I felt a hand on my back as I stared.

"What's up Snapps."

I swung around, "Akeisha, hey, how you doing?"

"I'd be better if you danced with me." This girl just wasn't going to stop I thought to myself. I decided one dance wasn't going to kill me, so I humored myself and led her to the dance floor. I kept a ruler distance between her and me, just in case she felt the urge to try and kiss me again or some shit. I didn't even bother to talk. I just sung the lyrics of the song in my head and waited for it to be over. I hated prom because they were going to play slow songs most of the damn night since it was majority couples in the room. I hoped Akeisha wasn't thinking she was going to be in my face all night. The instant the song ended I smiled and tried to walk away, but she grabbed me and hugged me tight. I let her get her hug in then I went on about my business.

An hour had gone by and another slow song was on. Rose walked over to me again smiling. "I saw you dance with Akeisha. That was sweet." She smiled.

"I was forced; you didn't see the gun in her hand?"

Rose laughed. "Well if you're done being held hostage I'm free to dance."

I stood and placed my hand on the small of her back to guide her to the dance floor. I pulled Rose as close as I could get her and she looked up into my eyes. I moved her body to the music to follow mine.

"And why are you staring at me?" Rose asked.

"You just look so good, excuse me for being inappropriate."

"So what I don't look good any other time?"

"Why do women always have to find the insult in compliments?"

"Why do *studs* refer to women as if they aren't women themselves?"

"Okay you got me there, but I'm just saying, you're beautiful all the time; you're just killing it tonight."

"Well thank you."

Rose smiled and laid her head in my chest. Three songs had played and we danced to each one. The last was *Starlight Gaze by Jas'mine Garfield*. I didn't want to let her go, but Greg came over and cut in during the last song. I decided to cut out of the dance at that moment.

"I'll see y'all at the hotel."

"Okay," Rose said as she hugged me. I head out of the dance and drove to the *Hilton* downtown.

I pulled up to the hotel and Rose called to inform me that she had invited Akeisha to chill with us. I already wasn't getting any ass that night and now she wanted to taunt me with the big girl who had been the bane of my existence for the last year or so. I took a deep breath and told myself to stop with the fat jokes in my head, because there were actually some big girls who could get it, especially those Jill Scott/Jennifer Hudson looking sisters and for damn sure Monique's big fine ass before the weight loss.

I sat in my car until Rose and Greg arrived then I walked into the lobby of the hotel to get my key. I gave Rose an ugly look when she approached.

She figured my words from my expression. "What was I supposed to do Snapps?"

I didn't respond and Rose rolled her eyes at me then went up to the room to wait for Akeisha. I stayed in the lobby to avoid her. She must have been waiting upstairs for us because Rose blew my cell phone up. I hit the reject button every time. I watched the elevators and finally Akeisha walked out. She exited the hotel and I was relieved. I went up to my room and Rose was heated.

"Snapps you are so fucking wrong."

"Wrong for what?"

"I was calling you!"

"And…"

"You could have at least come up to talk to her! I should call her back up."

"You do that and I'll just leave again and this time for good. Why you keep playing cupid anyway?"

"She's single and your single and you have *been* single, that's why!"

"Oh so since she's single and gay, you automatically assume that we are made for each other. FYI lesbians don't date each other just because they are gay. We do have types, just like straight people. Consider that your gay and lesbian lesson of the day," I shook my head thinking *fucking straight people to* myself.

"Well, excuse me for trying to help your lonely ass out."

"Here's an idea, don't!"

She sat silent for a moment then she looked up at me and spoke.

"So what is your type?"

I hesitated and swallowed back, "you…"

Rose fell silent again and this time I believe she was at a loss for words. I kneeled down in front of her and thought about how Lexi would clown me for what I was about to do. Lexi had been pushing me from the beginning to fuck Rose, turn her out, then bounce, but that just wasn't me. I guess I was the nice the guy and for that reason alone I kept finishing last, but I had hopes that Rose wouldn't put me in a losing space.

"Rose, you are the most beautiful woman I've ever seen in my life and since the day I laid eyes on you I've wanted you. I accepted being your friend because it was the only way for me to be near you. After that nigga fucked over you, you didn't want anything to do with anyone and I respected that, but shit it's been more than a year since then. He has moved on and so should you. You need to let someone in. Let me in. We both know you're just playing with Greg. Hell if you weren't you'd be in the room with him right now, but you're in here with me pretending to be mad."

Rose looked at me and placed her soft hands on each side of my face. She looked in my eyes to see if I was being sincere. If only she knew how real I was being at that moment. I swallowed back and then took the plunge and she allowed me to kiss her. She breathed hard as I worked her mouth with mine. I stopped and pulled myself back while her eyes remained closed. I stood up slowly in front of her just staring down at her. I pulled the bowtie from my neck and undid the first two buttons on my shirt and she stood to meet my gaze pulling my hands away from my shirt, undoing the remainder of my buttons and

75

pushing my shirt down my arms. We never broke our stare. I stared into her eyes wondering if I could figure out her thoughts.

Rose

It was part fascination and part curiosity that had me standing in front of Snapps. I had never kissed a girl before, never had the desire to. I thought maybe this attraction I was having to Snapps had a lot to do with her physical representation of a boy, but that thought soon cleared out when I pushed her shirt to the floor and pulled her sports bra up over her head. I had never touched anyone's breast that wasn't mine. I was unsure of what I should do. Did lesbians have sex the same way as straight people? Was I supposed to touch her as I would a man? Instead of figuring it out I kept my hands to myself. I knew what I liked and how I liked it…

****Snapps****

She unzipped her dress so that it could drop down to the floor and I unsnapped her strapless bra tossing it. I wondered if Greg would interrupt, but then I guessed he wouldn't if he figured Rose was in here playing matchmaker with Akeisha and me.

Rose's breast pointed at me and I grabbed them and put one into my mouth making sure she felt me as I pulled her nipple with the edges of my teeth, licking circles around it as she moaned. I sucked on

the other, giving each one equal attention. I licked
down the center of her body stopping at her belly ring
and pulling off her panties. She squealed as I wrapped
my lips around her pearl and sucked on it. Rose
couldn't stand any longer, so I laid her back on the
bed to continue what I was doing. I had to remove the
rest of my clothes because it was about to get serious.

Rose

My eyes were wide open as I stared at the
ceiling above us wondering how I got into this
position and how would I feel about it in the morning.
I curled my toes saying to myself that my body
should not feel this good and only a man was
supposed to make me feel this way. When Emmitt has
put his mouth on me for the first time I had to guide
his head it the right places, but here Snapps was
hitting all the right spots and making me feel as
though I wasn't going to last another minute. There
was no intensity, but it felt so good; it felt so different
and I felt relaxed.

Snapps

Rose had let me take complete control over
her body. I went as slow as possible since this was her
first time with a woman. The moment I felt she was
ready I eased my fingers into her, taking her by
surprise. Rose moaned and she kicked and she

screamed. She held on tight to my dreads until she came and I was satisfied that she was satisfied.

There was a knock on the room door the moment that we finished and laid in silence. Rose and I had gotten so wrapped in each other we forgot about everything and everybody else. Rose slipped out of bed with the sheet wrapped around her and walked to open the door. She swung it open and I heard Akeisha's voice, "Snapps, I know that," she paused in the middle of her love confession, "….Rose? What are you doing here? Am I in the wrong room?"

Akeisha must have looked down to see my white tuxedo pants on the floor and not the black ones that Greg was wearing, she pushed past Rose and I jumped up, pulling my bra over my head. "Bitch!" Akeisha charged at Rose, tearing into her. I ran to pull them a part. Greg heard all the commotion and ran out to see what it was. He saw Akeisha and Rose swinging at each other. Akeisha swung out of rage and Rose for defense. He didn't ask questions about me in my boxers and bra or Rose being naked. He just helped me pull them a part. Akeisha was getting the best of Rose, using her size to her advantage and slinging Rose into every wall available on the 24th floor. He drug Akeisha halfway up the hall once he finally got a good grip on her.

"Get out of here Akeisha before I call security!" Greg yelled. Akeisha shot one last look at Rose and I then stomped away. People poked their heads from their rooms to see what the commotion was. It was only a matter of time before Security came. We had to get out of there.

Greg turned around. "Y'all care to explain what the fuck is going on?" He asked then took one look at me and at Rose and finally put two and two together. Just like that, another heart was broken. He shook his head, pulled the room keys from his pocket and tossed it to Rose, then headed for the elevators.

Rose grabbed the sheet she was wrapped in from the floor and rushed back into the room to get dressed. I followed her lead grabbing my things. We rushed out of the room, leaving the keys on the dresser. The elevator was already on our floor, so we hopped on and hurried to the lot. We hopped into my rental and were out of there.

Rose and I sat in silence. I wanted to ask what was going through her head, but I knew that wasn't the right time since she had just had a fight with her best friend. Rose stared straight ahead barely blinking. "What now?" She finally spoke.

"We go on from here and talk about us."

"And Akeisha?"

"She'll be fine Rose. She knew I never wanted her. Your best friend would want what's best for you."

She nodded her head. "She's been my friend since we were eleven years old."

"She'll come around," I grabbed her hand and held it, smiling on the inside that I had finally had something my way for a change. It took me almost two years, but I got what I wanted and I wanted to be selfish for a second.

****Rose****

I tiptoed into the house not wanting my mother to question why I was home and not at my hotel. I held my arms around myself in shame that I had hurt my best friend. I went into my room and didn't bother turning on the light. I just hopped into my bed and laid there still in my dress. "I had sex with a girl," I said out loud to myself then laughed. I wasn't sure that I was supposed o enjoy it but I did and at the cost of my best friend. Akeisha was probably never going to speak to me again, but I couldn't let that happen because I had known her forever and she was the only real friend I believed myself to have. Each time I attempted to make friends with someone new they would get jealous of me and spread rumors about me. I trusted no one, but Akeisha, well until Snapps came along.

Somehow every thought that I had brought me right back to Snapps and it made me smile. I wanted whatever happened between us to happen again. I pulled out my phone and called her.

"Hello," she answered and now my smile was more intimate than friendly.

"How far are you?"

"Not too far?"

"Will you come back and lay with me?"

"What about your mom?"

"She's out like a light. She didn't even hear me come in. I'll open the back door for you and you can just come up."

"Alright see you in five."

I hung up and stood to remove my dress finally. I switched on the light and walked over to my mirror. Akeisha had busted my lip. I head to my bathroom to clean the cut then I headed downstairs to open the back door. When I got back upstairs I heard noise coming from my mother's room. I tiptoed over to her door then heard her silent moans. I turned up my face and moved quickly away from the door. I didn't remember seeing a car outside. She went to extremes to hide whoever this man was that she was seeing if he didn't even park out front.

After about ten minutes Snapps was creeping into my room. I was under my covers with nothing on. She undressed at the door leaving on her boxers and her sports bra. She eased into the bed with me and I pulled her close so that she could feel my warm, naked skin.

"Where are you clothes?" she whispered.

"Shhh," I said as I pulled her into me and eased my tongue into her mouth. I'd beg Akeisha for forgiveness later.

CHAPTER 8

Rose

Snapps and I looked at each other through the few people who sat between us for graduation. I blushed hard as she winked at me. I looked around for Akeisha but she was nowhere around. If I didn't feel bad before I was starting too. She was missing out on her high school graduation all because she didn't want to face me or Snapps. I hung my head until they finished speaking then I stood as they called our row up to get our diplomas.

I cried when the last name was called because I was officially an adult about to step into the real world. I pulled my hat from my head and held it up high as everyone else tossed theirs. I didn't want to lose it.

I found my mother after graduation to hug her and kiss her.

"I'm so proud of you baby," she smiled.

"Thank you," I said and smiled back.

"Go find your friends and meet me at the car so we can all go eat."

"Okay," I said and headed to search for Snapps through the crowd of families and friends. Snapps was easy to spot since she was tall. I pulled her arm to get her attention and turned around then reached back to hug me. "My mom is waiting for us." I said.

"Okay, mom I'm going to head out with Rose, we're going to eat dinner since you have to get to work."

"Okay sweetheart, have fun. We'll do something this weekend." Mrs. Adams said as she hugged Snapps and waved goodbye to me.

I pulled Snapps by the hand through the crowd then I dropped it once we got close to my mother's car. My mother made a lot of gay jokes but I still wasn't exactly sure how she would feel about me dating a girl. Snapps and I had just decided before graduation that we'd make it official and just give it a try. I had nothing to lose with trying. After Emmitt broke my heart, something different was exactly what I needed. Snapps made me feel good and there was no question about the attraction. I wasn't sure if it would ever be anything serious, but from our friendship alone it would be fun.

My mother started the car when we hopped in then she fought through the traffic and headed to *Olive Garden*. Snapps sat behind my mother and I stared at her through my peripherals from the passenger seat. I had to hold my smile so my mother wouldn't question me.

We pulled up to the restaurant and parked without a problem, but waiting was another story. We found a seat and waited for our names to be called.

"So Snapps are you going to a college?" my mother asked.

"Yes ma'am I am."

"Which one?" she pried further.

"I decided on Howard."

"HBCU, nice choice. You need to get Rose to leave Louisiana. This girl insists on LSU."

"Thank you and I've been trying Ms. Anderson. I don't know what else to do." Snapps said a little bit too flirtatiously for my mother.

The hostess called our name before she could question Snapps further and we headed to our table. Snapps and I sat beside one another in the booth and my mother sat on the other side. The hostess placed out menu's and started looking over them. Snapps and I whispered to each other about the menus unknowingly.

My mother cleared her throat, "Rose, Emmitt called. He wanted to congratulate you," she said as she looked over at Snapps for a reaction, but when she didn't get one she looked back down at her menu. "Where's Akeisha I thought she'd be here." My mother asked.

"She wasn't feeling too good"

"Mm so sad for her." She said nonchalantly. "Well, let's order and eat."

I sat looking at my mother, watching as she tried her hardest not to make eye contact with me or Snapps. I could tell she was uncomfortable. She had probably never been around someone gay this long in her life that wasn't a male hair dresser. I didn't understand how she could crack jokes and even let me sleepover at Snapps and still appear to be so uneasy. "Excuse me I 'm going to the restroom." I said then stood up.

Snapps stood up too. "I have to go too. I want to wash my hands before dinner."

I gave my mother an awkward smile then we headed off. I pushed the restroom door hard and Snapps followed me in.

"What's the matter?" Snapps asked.

"This...us...."

"What do you mean?"

"Look how my mother is looking at us."

"So"

"So? I don't know how my mother would feel if she knew what happened with us."

"I thought your mom was okay with gay people?"

"Most people are okay are gay people until someone close to them turns gay."

"Look just calm down, you're overreacting." Snapps placed her hands on my arms and rubbed them.

I took a deep breath, "maybe we should chill out for awhile. Akeisha already hates my guts. I can't have my mother treating me like an outcast right now."

"That's fine, whatever you want. I want you to be sure about what you're doing with me. You know I'd never try to force anything on you."

"I know. I'm just losing my shit with all this chaos." I took another deep breath then Snapps and I washed our hands and went back out to eat with my mother. I had a solid plan to get things back in order

with Akeisha and keep my mother from asking too
many questions.

Akeisha

Rose called twenty-three times and left several
voicemails, but I ignored every call and deleted the
messages without listening to them. I was pissed. I
hadn't left my room since everything happened with
her and me. I already knew she wanted to question
my whereabouts as if she had the right. I was sure her
mom was the one wondering where I was for the
dinner we had been planning for months before
graduation and I was positive she had not told her
mother why I was a no show. She called again and
finally I decided to pick up.

"Rose stop calling me!" I hung up the phone.
There was no explanation that she could give me for
what she had done. Sure I wasn't the smallest or the
prettiest girl walking, but I had a heart and a damn
good one. She was always in my way and for years I
never paid her getting more attention than me any
mind, but this was too far. My mind had traveled to
the darkest place that it could with thoughts of her
and Snapps. I felt silently tormented by their laughs. I
convinced myself that Rose had set this up from the
beginning and made me an inside joke for her and
Snapps to laugh at. I could easily ask what it was that
Rose had that I didn't, but I already knew.

"Akeisha!" My mom yelled from the front of
the house.

"What?!"

"Don't what me girl, I don't care if you are 18 I will still knock the teeth out of your mouth. Rose is at the door for you."

"I'm not here!"

"Get your black ass up here!"

I smacked my lips and walked to the door. Rose was standing there with a pitiful look on her face, holding her diploma. "If I'm not answering your phone calls what makes you think I want to see your face?"

"Showing up seems to be the only way to make you hear me." She closed the door behind her and I stomped back to my room while she followed. "Why weren't you at graduation?"

"You really have to ask?"

"Akeisha, I wasn't messing with Snapps."

"No, you were fucking her and all this time I thought you were strictly dickly and I thought you were my friend!"

"I am strictly dickly, well, I was. I don't know what happened. Snapps told me her feelings and everything just went on from there and you know you never have to question my friendship."

"Whatever Rose"

"Whatever nothing, we've been friends for years Kei; I won't just let our friendship end like this. I'm sorry."

I flopped down on my bed. "Sorry? You're always sorry Rose. Why did you keep lying to me telling me that Snapps was into me and she wasn't?"

"I didn't want to hurt your feelings."

"Oh and fucking her wouldn't hurt my feelings?"

"Akeisha stop bringing that up."

"How can I? Everybody loves Rose, oh Rose is this and Rose is that. I'll tell you what Rose is…a bitch!"

"I deserved that…"

"You deserve a lot more than that, but punching you in the face again won't satisfy me."

"You want me to stop seeing her Akeisha?" Rose moved to sit next to me on the bed.

I hated her being close to me because I wanted to hit her again. I felt that if she wasn't in the way I'd have Snapps by now and it would have been me in that room. I didn't want to give her my forgiveness. I didn't want to give her anything. I wanted her to leave.

"Kei…." She gave me a pitiful look then placed her hand on top of mine. "Just say the word and I'll leave her alone before anything more can happen."

I took a deep breath, "no, it's cool," I said hanging my head, "I was over it the night it happened. A part of me knew Snapps wouldn't go for someone like me anyway."

"So we're okay?"

"Yeah we're good"

"Can I hug you or are you going to hit me?"

I opened my arms and hugged Rose. I was still angry with her, but I couldn't' tell her that because all she would do was keep apologizing. Everybody thought Rose was little Ms. Perfect that could do no wrong and I was just the tag-a-long friend. She was no better than I was. I'd get the last laugh.

Snapps

After parting ways with Rose and her mother I hopped into my own car and decided to spend some time with myself and get a head start on breathing "real world air". My mother would always say real world air because she believed all teens lived in a different reality than adults since we had nothing to worry about at our age. I wanted to be close to water so I decided to drive to the lake.

I sat on the lakefront in my car staring out at the water. Everyone else was out celebrating graduation while I was looking back at all that I had accomplished and all that was to come. I was satisfied with the dinner that I had with Rose and her mom. I smiled and leaned my seat back.

The default ringtone on my phone sounded and I wondered who it was. It was a California number. "Hello" I said into the phone, but no one said anything back. "Hello!" I said again louder this time.

"Sasha?"

"Granny?"

"The one and only."

My heart sped up in my chest. I knew that lady's voice from anywhere. She was the only woman that could call me Sasha other than my mother and get away with it. I had not spoken with my grandmother since my father passed away. My mother had gone into hiding after his death and cut off his entire side of the family. His parents hated my mother until I came along. "How'd you get my number?"

She laughed, "I'm 72 years old, I know a few things."

I smiled and my eyes started to water, "How are you?"

"I'm great baby, I still feel thirty-five." She joked.

"How's granddad?"

"He's just fine dear." We both sat silent. "Congratulations on graduating. You're a big girl now.

"Yes ma'am I'm a big girl now." I laughed.

"Tell me about yourself, what all have a missed?"

"Well, I've been accepted in several colleges, I met a nice girl, and…"

My grandmother cleared her throat, "A nice girl?"

I closed my eyes tight and cussed at myself. I was going to give my grandmother a heart attack. I don't hear from her in years and the first thing I blurt out id that I'm gay. I shook my head at myself, "yes ma'am a girl."

"Well that's just lovely."

"Really?"

"Yes sweetheart. It's your life. I'm just glad to be hearing your voice." My grandmother started to laugh at my shock. "You know it's funny how people live most of their lives worried about someone else's then they wonder where theirs went."

"I agree granny."

"So are you the boy or the girl in the relationship?"

I laughed, "we're both girls."

"Well, I know that, but who's the more masculine one?"

"I guess I am."

"I'm not surprised. You were an aggressive child."

I laughed.

"Well, I know it's late there and I have to give your granddad his insulin. Save my number and you call me anytime you hear me."

"Yes ma'am" I said as a single tear fell down my face. I was so happy.

CHAPTER 9

Snapps

It was a hot summer and I was wrapping my mind around being a college freshman in two and a half months. It was back to being a part of the youngest class in school all over again, but I didn't mind the change to come. I hadn't talk to Rose in days. I was giving her space since the whole Akeisha incident and her mother prying at dinner. It was hard to tell if she would be okay with us or not so I just kept my distance. I was missing Rose though so I figured a phone call wouldn't hurt anything. I pulled my phone from my pocket and dialed her up.

"Hello," She picked up all jolly.

"In a good mood?" I asked.

"Actually I am."

"May I ask why?"

"I don't know, I'm free from high school hell, I can party legally, my best friend is speaking to me again, and you just called and made me smile instantly, pick one." Rose giggled.

"Akeisha finally answered your call?"

"No, I showed up at her door after our graduation dinner."

"What did she say?"

"She forgave me. I really hope she isn't mad at me anymore."

"Who cares if she's mad; I really don't know why she's your friend."

"You sound like my mother."

"Damn moms don't like her? That should be a sign." I said, but then decided I didn't want to get into details, because then I'd have to explain that dinner date disaster and everything Akeisha said about Rose. For some reason all I saw was Rose getting angry with me."Anyways am I seeing you later, it's been damn near a week?"

"Yeah I have to make a quick run to the store since I have my mom's car. I have to go back to the house and meet her so we can go shopping. She wants to get an early start on getting my stuff for my dorm."

"Sounds like she trying to get rid of you if you ask me. You have like two and a half months ma."

"Shut up Snapps. I'll scoop you up on my way from the store."

"Oh you're taking me along with you and moms to shop?" I joked.

"Yeah I called up some old boys I used to kick it with to get them to start ringing the phone again and it killed her suspicion." Rose laughed.

I smiled half-way okay with her scam and half-way disturbed by it, wondering if she actually sat and chit chatted with those cats. "Okay, well, I'm about to shower and shit, buzz me when you're outside love."

94

"Okay babe."

"Wait, what'd you call me?"

"Babe." I could tell she was smiling.

"I like the sound of that. See you in a few."

I hung up the phone to toss on some clothes and let her handle her business.

Rose

Everything was perfect in my life now. Akeisha had forgiven me, Snapps was a love that I could trust, and I was soon to be a hot college girl just like I had always dreamed. There was nothing that could get in my way now. I pulled up to Snapps house and called her phone to let her know that I was outside. She didn't answer so I called again. The phone went straight to voicemail the second time. I called one more time and if she didn't answer I was going to drive off.

"Hello."

"You didn't see me calling?"

"You know I always have my iPod going."

"Yeah okay bring your ass."

"Alright." She hung up the phone. It took her about three minutes to get out of the house and hop into the car with me. "Hey beautiful, she smiled at me."

"Hey." I smiled back then put the car in drive and headed home.

"Can I ask you something?" Snapps inquired.

"Yeah, what?"

"You feel okay about this whole situation?"

"What situation"

"Dating a girl?"

"Yeah, why?"

"I don't know, most so-called straight girls usually run back to niggas after awhile."

"Why would I do that?"

"You might eventually feel like this isn't the life for you."

"I'm happy Snapps. I sometimes don't understand what I'm feeling because most of my life I was taught being with men was normal and natural, but being with you feels the exact same way."

"That's all I needed to hear." Snapps smiled.

I pulled into my driveway and grabbed my purse from the backseat. "Why in the world is my front door opened. I could have sworn my mama closed it after I left."

"Maybe she never did."

"Probably not, she was in the tub when I left." I walked inside and sat my purse on the end table by the door. "MOM!" I yelled through the house, but she didn't respond. I walked over to the phone to check if we had any missed calls, but it read zero. "Mommy!"

"She might be upstairs getting dressed and can't here you." Snapps suggested.

I placed the phone back down in the console and ran up the stairs to my mother's bedroom, but it was empty. It was too quiet. I walked into her bathroom and everything with black.

Snapps

"Rose you good up there?" I looked up when I heard a loud thud against the floor. Rose didn't respond so I walked up the stairs to find her. I walked into her mother's bedroom and saw Rose passed out on the floor between the bedroom and the bathroom. I ran over to her. "Rose baby get up." I looked over at the tub and jumped back. "Holy shit!" I pulled my cell phone from my pocket and called 911.

"911, what's your emergency."

"My girlfriend is passed out on the floor and her mother is dead in the bathtub!"

"Are you sure she's dead did you check her pulse?"

"Her head is under water and she's damn near blue!"

"I'm sending a unit right now ma'am I need you to stay on the line with me."

I shook my head yes as if the operator could see me. She asked question after question, but I couldn't say a single word as I looked over at Rose's mother lying in the bathtub dead, topless with jeans on. There was blood down the shower tile so either she fell and hit her head or someone had banged her head against that wall. I tried to look around at something she could have possibly slipped on. My mind was racing and my body was shaking.

Rose's eyes fluttered opened and I dropped the phone from my ear and crawled over to her. "Rose get up baby, come over here." I tried to pull her back before she could lay eyes on the body again,

97

but I didn't move her fast enough. She started to scream. She screamed so loud my ears vibrated. Rose crawled over to the tub where her mother was, pulling her body from the water. "No, no, no, no, no," she cried, "who did this to you," tears fell down her eyes as she pulled her mother from the tub, "HELP ME! HELP ME Snapps!" She screamed and held her mother's body close to her, rocking. I was frozen in place. Snot ran down her nose and her tears were endless. The ambulance and police rushed in after what seemed like forever. Rose fought them as they tried to pry her mother from her arms. This shit was unreal. "Snapps! Don't let them take her! No!!!" I walked over and wrapped my arms around her tight and held her as they prepared a body bag for her mother.

"Shhhh, it's okay." I said as I stroked her hair and watched them pack her mother away like produce. I walked with Rose out of the room and down the stairs as they carried her mother out. Two Police Officers stood out front talking to neighbors as we exited the house. An old lady pointed at Rose saying 'that's her daughter right there.' The detectives walked over to us.

They stopped in front of us and pulled out their badges. The female cop spoke first. "I'm detective Shelby Stone and this is my partner Ryan King. I know this may be difficult right now, but I need you to answer a few questions Ms?

Rose turned around with bloodshot eyes. "Rose, Rose Anderson."

"Ms. Anderson were you the one who discovered the body?"

"Yes, but I passed out," Her voice cracked.

"So who called 911?"

"I did," I chimed in. "I heard her fall so I ran up the steps."

"Do you know of anyone who would want to hurt your mother? A Co-worker, a friend?" Detective King finally spoke.

"No, nobody"

"Was she dating anyone?"

"There was a guy, but I never met him or saw him. She never introduced me to her male friends unless she was going to keep them.

They jotted down notes in a notebook then Detective Stone looked at Detective Shelby. "Get the entire house searched. Look for old phone books and her cell phone. Dust everything, see if we can get an I.D. on the boyfriend, maybe a neighbor has seen him before and can get us a description." Detective King walked away to do as Shelby instructed.

"Here is my card and if I have any more questions I'll be contacting you." Detective Stone informed. "Do you have somewhere to stay for the night?" She asked.

"She can stay with me." I answered. I looked over at Rose then placed my hands on her shoulders. "Stay right here, I'll get you some things." She nodded her head and I walked back into the house. This shit was unreal was the only thought in my head. I was freaking out inside, but I had to remain calm for Rose.

I packed a bag for Rose just grabbing a few shirts, some pants, and panties. We could worry about the rest of her things later. I took the keys to her mom's car and we rode back to my house in complete silence. I pulled up in front of my house and parked then helped Rose from the passenger seat. She was still shook up. My mother was sleep when we got inside so I made sure I was quiet. I was going to ask Rose if she wanted to take a bath, but I was sure a tub was the last thing she wanted to see at the moment so I just laid her out across my bed and pulled my covers over her. I removed my shoes and hopped in bed beside her without getting undressed.

"What am I going to do now?" She asked in a whisper.

"Whatever you have to…"

"She's really gone Snapps." Rose said somberly.

"Yeah…" I said as I placed my hand on her cheek.

"I won't be able to pay for school or come home to visit for the holidays…" tears started to form in her eyes. "She was my only family. Why would someone do this?"

"I wish I had an answer." I pushed her hair from her face, "just try to get some sleep, we'll figure everything out okay. I'm not going to leave your side, I promise," I kissed her forehead. I had to come up with a plan.

CHAPTER 10

Snapps

The church was dreary as the pastor went on and on about Rose's mother and how much of a great woman she was. Rose could not stop crying. I knew exactly how she felt because of my own experience with loss, but all I could do was sit there, rub her back, and pray that was enough.

Akeisha sat at the back with dark shades over her eyes looking unaffected. She sat very still as if funerals were something that she attended often. A guy a few pews up from Akeisha kept staring at Rose and I. He was the same color as a cocoanut, his hands were big, and you could see his muscles bulging through his shirt. I took a guess that he was Rose's ex-boyfriend because of his physical build. It made me uneasy knowing that he was sitting right there, but this was no time to be petty or even a hint of jealous when I was the one sitting beside her.

Rose gripped my hand almost cutting off my circulation as she grieved and fought to hold herself together. "Cry baby, its okay." I whispered into her ear and just as I ended the sentence a loud shriek flew from her pink lips. She folded over, shaking uncontrollably as if there were chills from a bad fever coursing through her body. I rubbed her back some more. I wasn't going to leave her side.

The pastor spoke his last piece then everyone started to stand to view the body one last time. Rose stood and I stood right behind her, being her shadow, nipping at her heels. She walked slower than I had ever seen anyone walk before. It was as if her feet were wrapped in cement. I wasn't sure that she would make it to the coffin, but she did. She leaned down in the coffee touching her mother's cold skin and kissing her on the forehead. She was stronger than me, because I would have passed out; just standing so close to her mother's dead body was making me nauseous when I had just seen her full of life a week ago.

Rose fell to her knees the instant she walked away from the coffin that would shut off the very last vision she had of her mother, leaving her with echoes of her laughter and blurs of her smile. My heart was broken for her.

The grave site was even worse. Everyone fell apart. If I could have opted out I would have. I thanked God when it was over.

I sat in a corner in a little blue chair in Rose's house, watching her from afar as person after person hugged and kissed her, telling her they were sorry for her loss. From where I sat it seemed like every hug was a blow to the chest and every kiss was the hit of reality that her mother was really gone.

I sat straight up in my seat the instant the dude I guessed was her ex walked over to pull her into a tight embrace that last a bit longer than it needed to. I clenched my jaw and balled my fist, but I sat still. It was just a hug. I saw him whispering something into her ear, she nodded her head and he walked away. I stood and walked over to her, placing my hand on the same place it had been since this all began, her back. I was almost ready to permanently glue it there if it would keep her comforted forever. "Are you good?" I asked more concerned about what ole boy had just said to her than what she might be feeling.

She didn't say a word. She just nodded like she had been doing for the past week with everyone. She didn't have very many words, only gestures. There was so much that she had to take on in such a short time. She found out that her mother was up to her neck in debt trying to stash away money to put her through college since she wasn't awarded a scholarship. The house was being put up for auction in two days and she'd have to find a new place to live.

People started leaving the house around six that evening, hugging and kissing Rose one last time and telling her to call them if she needed anything, of course to me that was just something to say, because nobody ever really had anything to offer you other than false affection. They'd all go on with their lives within twenty-four hours and Rose's mother would be a painless memory for them. They felt sorry for you for that moment then it passed.

I closed the door behind the guest once the last one was gone and looked around for Rose, but she had vanished. I knew exactly where she was.

Rose

Everything was a blur to me as I sat in the same bathroom where my mother took her last breath. I held her shirt up against my face, trying to force the memory of her scent into my mind permanently. I was tired of crying and tired of wondering who would do something so cruel. The police said they were doing all that they could, but I knew better. They were doing the exact opposite.

I felt empty inside and not because my mother was gone, but because I would probably never see justice. At first they wanted it a suicide, but from the angle she laid and the place on the wall where the blood trickled it was ruled a homicide.

Tap Tap

I jumped up to see Snapps standing in the doorway. "You okay in here?"

"Yeah, I'm okay."

"Everybody is gone. You want to come back to my place or do you want to stay here."

"I think I'll stay here the next two nights, before it belongs to the bank."

"You want me to stay with you?"

"No, I think I need to deal with this alone for awhile."

"Okay. Call me if you need me?"

"I will and thank you for everything." I walked over to Snapps to give her a tight, long hug. "Let me walk you to the door."

I escorted Snapps downstairs to the door then kissed her and waved goodbye. I waited until she pulled off then walked to the back door and opened it. "Emmitt?You out here?" Emmitt stepped out of the shadows.

"Everyone gone?"

"Yeah?"

"And your little girlfriend?"

"Yeah."

"I leave for a year and you turn gay on me. Did I hurt you that bad?"

"Bad enough," I hung my head.

"Let me make it up to you then," He pushed me back into the house, pushing the door shut with his foot and placed his hands on my face. His presence was still familiar to me as he pressed his lips against mine and awakened the same teenage girl that he had deflowered years ago. I needed a commonplace to fill the hole inside the great loss I had suffered and Emmitt was exactly it. I pushed thoughts of Snapps as far back in my mind as I could although I knew it was wrong. I just wanted to be selfish for a moment and trust that what she would never know could never hurt her. Memories of Emmitt and I sneaking around when my mother was asleep in the next room, drown me as she swirled his tongue around in my mouth and gripped my back firmly. The adrenaline would always get me going as I wondered if my mother would walk in at any second and catch her "innocent" baby-girl on her back, legs

105

in the air, being mounted by the boy she always had so much respect for.

I had been dealing with an excruciating pain that entire week and I just wanted it to go away. Emmitt lifted me up carrying me to the living room and tossing me down on the sofa as he ripped off his shirt, popping every last button on the crisp white button down that he wore. He kneeled down in front of me. "Is this how dykes do it?" He pushed the ugly black funeral skirt up above my waist and pushed his mouth against my panties nibbling on my clit through the material, then pulling it to the side with his teeth and sliding his tongue across my lower lips. I dug my nails into the sofa and closed my eyes, but Snapps' face flashed and they popped back open. Now was not the time to feel guilty I said to myself and shut my eyes again to be taken to a familiar place by Emmitt.

"I want you inside me Emmitt." I pulled his head up and forced off his pants. I needed him now, before I let the guilt stop me.

"Let me get a condom."

"No, just pull out before you cum," I whined like a child, "do it now."

Emmitt didn't protest as he whipped out the part that used to invade me so generously. I screamed out into the air as his muscles flexed and dominated my petite frame. I took all of him into me as I temporarily forgot about all my duress. I'd let tomorrow worry about itself.

CHAPTER 11

Snapps

My mother stomped up the stairs behind me after receiving the news that I wouldn't be taking any of the out-of-state college offers or scholarships. "You have seriously lost your fucking mind if you think I worked hard to watch you throw away your future for some trick!"

"She's not a trick, she's my girlfriend." I said out loud claiming something I didn't even know for sure myself.

"Sasha she was just jumping on dick a few months ago? Do you seriously think that little girl cares about you?"

"She does mama and she needs me right now. I can't just abandon her, where will she go?"

"I don't give a fuck where she goes!"

"Her mother just died!"

"That's not your problem and you better stop screaming at me! You can still get stomped in here little girl."

I took a deep breath and sighed, "Ma I'm just saying, maybe one or two years at a community college or something until she gets on her feet then I'll take another offer."

"I can't believe this."

"I'm eighteen and it's my decision."

My mother shook her head and walked off. I would have thought she would understand what it felt like to be abandoned after my father died without a will or insurance left behind. I'd never let Rose struggle like that. I was better than that.

Rose

I turned over in my bed and Emmitt was snoring loudly like he had not slept in days. I eased out of bed and picked up my cell phone, carrying it into the bathroom with me and dialing Akeisha's number. I put the toilet seat down and sat on top of it while I waited for her to answer.

"Hello."

"Hey Kei, I need to talk."

"What's wrong? Nightmare?"

"No, I think I cheated on Snapps."

"What do you mean you think? Are y'all official?"

"I think so, I mean she's been around this whole time...I...we never said it out loud..."

"Okay, stop, just tell me what happened."

"I did it with Emmitt last night."

"You little tramp. What happened?"

"I don't know. I just know I needed him to be around last night. I mean I care about Snapps, but

Emmitt is so familiar to me right now. I feel like I just need any type of normalcy I can get right now."

"I'm shaking my head over here."

"Don't judge me right now please."

"No judgment from over here baby, but you better be careful, we gays don't play that straddling the fence shit."

I sighed. "I know."

"So do you want to be with him?"

"No, I want to be with Snapps, I just needed to be dominated. I felt so helpless."

"Snapps could have done that."

"No she couldn't, she's so gentle and passionate."

"What's wrong with that?"

"Nothing, I just didn't want that…"

"I'm shaking my head again, but your secret is safe with me. He'll be gone back to school soon anyway. Use his ass while he's here then drop him like a bad habit the same way he did you."

I laughed for the first time in days. "It would be nice to see him suffer." Akeisha and I laughed a little bit more then I hung up the phone and went back into the bedroom and Emmitt was awake. "Hey, how long you been up?"

"I just opened my eyes, waiting for you to come out of the bathroom so I can drain the main vein."

"Ewgo ahead."

Emmitt laughed and I crawled back into bed to catch up on all the sleep I had lost.

****Snapps****

I applied at several places for a job. I was starting to wish I had worked in fast food or something while I was in high school so I could at least have a work history. I really didn't want to be flipping burgers, but I didn't have many options and no way to show I had many skills.

I drove past a gas station that had help wanted hanging on the door, so I busted a "U" and pulled into the lot. I hopped out and walked inside to speak with an attendant, possibly a manager. "Hey how old do you have to be to work here?" I asked.

"At least eighteen."

"What are the requirements?"

"No experience is really needed, we'll send you to a class to get you certified to sell tobacco and all that good stuff and we train for free."

"May I have an application?"

"Yeah, sure," the attendant smiled at me and pulled the application from behind the desk and handed it over to me. I pulled a pen from my pocket and moved to the side to complete it so I didn't block the customers. I finished it in ten minutes then walked back over to the attendant. I felt like she was kind of flirting with me. She kept smiling and making eyes at me. She took my application and told me to wait as she walked to the back.

A heavy set white man walked out front with my application in his hands. He walked over to me and reached out his hand introducing himself. "Gene Chapman."

"Sasha Adams." I matched his firm grip as I returned the greeting.

"Let's just skip the casualties. I just fired three people and I need bodies like yesterday, Can you do double shifts?"

"Yes sir?"

"We'll do all your official paperwork later and I'll just pay you in cash until you're processed."

"When can you start?"

"Asap!"

"Alright be here tomorrow morning in a black shirt and some nice pants, khakis if you have them."

"Thank you so much!" I shook his hand one more time then rushed out to my car to call my mom and Rose to tell them the good news. I was sure my mom wouldn't be so thrilled, but she had to respect my decision.

Rose

"What took you so long to answer the phone?" Snapps asked as I watched Emmitt dress himself in the corner of my bedroom.

"I was in the shower baby and didn't hear the phone."

"Oh, you had my nerves bad."

"You have to stop worrying about me, I'm okay, I promise."

"That's good to know. I just wanted to tell you my good news."

"What is it?"

"I got a job!"

"You what? Why?"

"So I can take care of us."

"Snapps you didn't have to do that. I want you to go to school."

"I can go to school here. I told you I wasn't leaving your side."

"You are just too good you know that?"

"I know it, but look I'm headed back home to tell my mom, whenever you're ready for me to come help you pack up the house just hit me up okay?"

"Okay baby," I hung up the phone and held it close to my chest. I had completely forgotten that Emmitt was still in the room.

"So you moving in with the dyke huh?"

"Where else am I supposed to go?"

"You could come with me."

"And sleep in a twin bed in a square room with a shared bathroom? I'll pass…"

Emmitt laughed and shook his head. "I'm going to keep my comment to myself right now since the last thing I want to do is fight with you while you're grieving. I have a few things to handle before I leave, so I'll see you later. You really need to consider coming with me."

"I'll think about it."

"Think hard."

Emmitt walked over and pulled me into his arms and kissed my cheek. I loved seeing him sweat.

THREE MONTHS
LATER

CHAPTER 12

Rose

    Emmitt was pissed off when I chose to stay with Snapps. He refused to believe that my feelings for Snapps were stronger than my feelings for him since he and I had "history". It was the little girl in me that longed for him and after accepting the reality that my mother really wasn't coming back I accepted that I was a different person and Snapps was the fresh start that I needed. She did anything I asked her too and she loved me more than anyone ever had. I was still fucking Emmitt from time to time, but we were on pause at the moment since he was in his feelings about the situation.

    "Do you have to leave your shoes in the exact spot that you take them off? You really had me fooled thinking you were a neat and tidy girl when I first met you, placing your stuff to the side and shit when you first slept over…" Snapps interrupted my thoughts.

    "Oh shut up because you drop your clothes everywhere."

"At least they aren't in places that my mother can complain about them."

"You're mother complains about everything."

"That's true." We both fell into laughter at the thought of her mother nagging us about every little thing from placing a coaster under our glasses to not leaving clothes in the dryer. Snapps walked over to me and pecked my lips. "I have to get to work, you good?"

"Yeah."

"Must be nice to be able to sit in your girlfriend's bed all day and paint your toes and shit."

"Yeah but look at the cost, my mother had to pass away and after paying off her debts I'm going to need a job soon."

"You need to get into school, let me worry about the finances."

"You get a small promotion at work and you start feeling yourself."

"Don't be a hater baby; it's really not a good look on you."

"Whatever, go to work," I kissed her once more then popped her on the butt as she walked away shaking her head. She hated that, but I got a kick out of it. I sat in the bed until I heard the front door shut then I counted to sixty before grabbing the cigarettes I had hidden in my bottom drawer. I walked to the backyard to smoke. It wasn't a habit that I was proud of, but I had to keep my nerves calm somehow. I took a seat in the patio chair that Ms. Adams had in the backyard and lit my cigarette. I puffed it maybe three times before I was interrupted.

"Snapps know you hitting those cancer sticks?" Ms. Adams asked.

"No, I'm sure she wouldn't approve."

"Those things will kill you."

"I'm well aware of that."

"Mmm hmm." Ms. Adams said as she closed the door back. I thought I heard her squeeze out the word tramp too, but I was in no mood to acknowledge her. She eyed me daily and I wasn't sure I could blame her. If I had a daughter like Snapps who was smart and sweet, I'd be unhappy with her decisions too and the girl who encouraged them even if it was silently. I wanted to move out, but I was waiting on the right time to tell Snapps. I figured she might get angry with me if I suggested we leave her mother alone. I pulled my cell phone from my pocket and called Akeisha.

"Hey skeezer." She said as she picked up the phone.

"Hey lint licker."

"Not funny, wassup?"

"Nothing sitting outside smoking."

"You're already skinny, those things are going to make you disappear."

"Oh well, they keep me calm."

"Weed can keep you calm."

"Never tried it."

"Shit I'm about to roll-up right now."

"Since when do you smoke?"

"Since I graduated and started living in reality."

"I feel that, well why don't you come scoop me up?"

117

"Okay I'll be there in ten."

Snapps

I stocked shelf after shelf waiting until it was time for me to get off. I was the only person at work and it was slow as hell so the time was creeping. I heard the bell ring at the door which meant a customer had walked it. I looked up from stocking to see my ex Anya walking in. I stood and walked to the front counter. "What can I do for you?"

"Sasha…Adams…," she said my name slowly.

"Don't call me that."

"My bad Snapps, how you been?"

"Good, what you need?"

"Aww don't be like that. I see you still looking good."

"Thanks."

"Still with umm what's her face, Daisy?"

"It's Rose… and yes I'm still with her. How do you even know I'm dating her."

"I hear things."

"Yeah, whatever. You still with your busted ex?"

"Actually we broke up."

"Good for you."

"We should hang out sometimes, you know catch up."

"Or not."

"I don't remember you being so mean."

118

"I guess you don't remember the naked pictures in your phone you were sending to every Tom, Dick, and Harry either, or the text message telling your ex bitch I was just something to do."

"You have to stop living in the past. We were kids Snapps. Look," she reached for my cell phone in my front pocket and pulled it out, "this is my number and whenever you just want to chit chat, call me, no drama, no bullshit, promise." she placed my phone back in my pocket then handed me thirty dollars. "Pump two sexy." She winked and walked away.

Anya had picked up some weight and I knew it wasn't from hamburgers because it was all in the hips and ass. A nigga was hitting that shit. I shook my head at how fine she was. She had always been a curvy girl, but those curves had grown up. I had to shake my head at myself just because I couldn't stop looking. I punched in her numbers for her pump then placed her money in the drawer and got back to what I was doing.

Akeisha

Rose and I passed blunts back and forth in my car. She choked for awhile, but got hooked to the high quickly. "Bitch we need some drinks." I suggested.

"We really do, but who's going to get us some?" Rose asked with her eyes low. "And you were right, weed is better than cigarettes. I feel crazy as a motherfucka, but good." She giggled.

"Call Emmitt, he can get us some liquor, ain't he twenty-one?"

119

"He is, but I think he gone though."

"Call and find out."

Rose pulled her phone out and called Emmitt. "Baby where are you?"

"Oh I'm baby now?"

"You know you're always going to be my baby."

"Yeah uh huh, what you need?"

"Are you here?"

"I never left."

"What?"

"I sat the semester out. I needed some time off after the shit you dropped on me."

"Don't start with me E, just come bring some drinks to Akeisha's crib, we sitting in her car."

"What y'all want?"

"Whatever you buy."

"Okay I'll be there in a few."

Rose hung up with Emmitt and we got back to the blunts.

It took Emmitt about twenty minutes to get to us with the drinks. He hopped in my back seat and pulled out some plastic cups. "Say is your mom home?"

"Hell no nigga I'd be parked somewhere else."

"Okay cool, I just didn't want her to come out here wigging out."

"My mom probably would join in." We all laughed. It was just like old times with a bit more illegal activity involved.

Snapps

I walked into the house exhausted, dropping my keys at the door then dragging my feet up the stairs. I walked into my bedroom and switched on the light and it was empty. I thought Rose would have been sleeping at least, where the hell could she be at eleven o'clock at night? I walked into my mom's room. "Mom do you know where Rose is?"

"She left with her friend Akera, Akenya, hell something."

"Akeisha." I laughed. "Alright, thanks." I pulled her door and she yelled through it.

"That girl been smoking cigarettes you know."

I pushed the door back open. "Huh?"

"Yep, caught her in the backyard today; I'm trying to tell you what you dealing with Sasha. This girl just lost her mother, she is not that little girl you were crushing on anymore."

"Mom…"

"I said my peace baby, that's all."

I pulled the door shut again then pulled my phone from front my pocket to call Rose. Her phone went straight to voicemail several times, so I called Akeisha's phone. Somebody had better answer.

Akeisha

I stared at Emmitt and Rose in my backseat as they swapped DNA through the mouth, just being

121

around the bitch lowered my self-esteem and I was a pretty cocky bitch. I found myself asking the same questions I had been asking since prom night. Why her? Why is it always her that gets what I want? Even though I didn't want Emmitt I was pretty sure if I did she would have dug her claws into him before I could even think about it. Light skinned bitch! I wondered if she only hung with me because she knew she looked better and could take all the attention. My thoughts were getting the best of me as I conjured up evil plan after evil plan to get to Snapps and make Rose out to be exactly what she was, a ho. My cell phone lit up in my cup holder. I smiled when I saw the name on the screen.

"I have to take this outside of the car. It's my mom."

"Okay," Rose said as she continued to let her hormones rage against Emmitt.

"Wassup Snapps?"

"Rose with you?"

"Yeah she's right here."

"Let me holla at her."

"She's kind of occupied right now."

"What you mean she occupied?"

"She's doing something."

"Man Kei don't play with me bruh, put her on the phone."

"I can't."

"Alright then cool, I'm on my way." Snapps hung up in my face and I smiled. I opened the car door and peeked,"I gotta run in the house and handle something for my mom, and y'all try not to get y'all fluids on my seats." Emmitt waved me off as he pulled one of Rose's nipples from beneath her shirt and pulled it into his mouth. I shut the door and skipped inside. I went up to my room and sat by the window, waiting.

My skin tingled as Emmitt's tongue ran up and down my neck. I wasn't sure if he had just gotten better at what he did or if the weed was enhancing the feeling. Whatever it was I was enjoying it and I was glad Akeisha had something to do, so she wouldn't be sitting here watching us. I didn't need an audience. Emmitt couldn't take the teasing anymore and moved me from on top of him. "Lay back," he commanded and I did as I was told. I guessed he wasn't upset with me anymore. Just as I leaned my head against the window the glass shattered behind his head and I heard Snapps' voice.

"This is what you do while I'm at work?!"

"Shit! Snapps, calm down," I jumped up, pulling my shirt down.

"Calm down?! You in the backseat with your ex and you want me to calm down?"

"Baby, I know what it looks like."

"Looks like I should bust you upside your fucking head, get out of the fucking car!"

Emmitt swung the car door open and hit Snapps with it and she fell to the ground, dropping the crowbar she was holding in her hand. Emmitt stood over her and picked her up by her neck then punched her hard. "I can't stand you fucking gay hos,

123

walking around here dressed like niggas, but can't even handle yourself."

"Emmitt stop it!"

"Stop? She busted glass over my fucking head."

"Please Emmitt please."

Emmitt continued to choke Snapps and she was becoming weak, so I jumped on his back and he knocked me off then dropped Snapps on the ground. She gasped for air and blood ran from her lip as she tried to breathe. "You jumping on me for this bitch? You must really love her, well if you love her so much tell her you're pregnant."

Snapps held her hand around her throat, rubbing it and looked over at me. "You what?"

Emmitt walked over to me and kicked me hard in the stomach, "The stupid bitch is pregnant." I held my stomach and Snapps stood up to run up on Emmitt again, but he punched her and knocked her back down. She grabbed the crowbar when she fell and jumped up again, hitting him hard in the back of the leg as he walked away, making him fall to his knees. "Pussy!" She yelled. "Make you feel good to punch and kick girls?!" She lifted the crowbar to hit him over the head, but Akeisha finally ran outside to stop her as I yelled.

"Snapps no!" I screamed in agony.

Emmitt stood slowly and walked to his car then sped off, leaving behind tire marks and the smell of burnt rubber.

"What the fuck happened?!" Akeisha asked.

"You know exactly what happened, fuck you." Snapps limped to her car and Akeisha ran over to me.

"Snapps help me," Akeisha yelled.

"Fuck both of y'all"

"Snapps she's bleeding, please!"

Snapps walked over to me and saw that blood was seeping through my jeans. She helped Akeisha lift me into the backseat and they rushed me to the hospital.

Snapps

I sat in the waiting room staring at my ex's number in my phone. I needed somewhere to go where nobody could find me. I stood up and walked toward the exit.

"Where you going?" Akeisha asked.

"Mind my business."

She stood and ran after me. "Snapps wait."

"What Akeisha?"

"I'm sorry. I thought you needed to know."

"You could have just told me over the phone, look at my face Akeisha."

"You wouldn't have believed me, I'd just look like the bitter friend. You needed to see for yourself." She placed her hands against my chest, sliding them up slowly to my shoulders. "You are so much better than what Rose has to offer right now."

I snatched her hands away from me by her wrist. "Don't ever fucking touch me," I walked off mumbling, "fucking Precious slash Rasputia look alike tryna push up on me, what the fuck wrong with that ho?" I pushed the exit doors hard and called information to get a number for a cab company since I left my car in front of Akeisha's door.

The cab pulled up in ten minutes then I dialed Anya to get her address. I was in no mood to pick up my car and revisit that scene.

The cab driver attempted to make conversation, but I wasn't in the mood. I stared out of the window until we pulled up to Anya's crib. I tossed him twenty dollars and hopped out. "Keep the change," I said shutting the door behind me. Anya opened the door with a smiled on her face before I could even knock. "I knew you would… what the fuck happened to your face?"

"I don't want to talk about it."

"If it has anything to do with that bitch I'll…"

"Anya stop with the concerned ex act and just get me something to clean my face with."

Anya didn't protest. She did as I suggested while I took a seat on her sofa. She returned with peroxide, cotton balls, and a little box of band aids. She sat everything on her coffee table then started to examine the cuts on my face. She soaked a cotton ball with peroxide a pressed it to the side of my lip.

"Ouch!"

"Quit flinching, I have to clean it so it doesn't get infected." Anya said as she dabbed the cuts.

"Don't press on it so hard."

She placed a band aid over my eye and leaned back beside me, "you should probably take that shirt off."

"And wear what?"

"Nothing, I've seen you naked before Sasha. You forget I knew you when you still owned girl underwear."

"Bring that up again and I'll hurt you."

"I'll just punch you in the other eye." She smiled.

"Haha."

"Come on seriously, take this off," she leaned in, rubbing her hand across my chest. Damn she was fine. I had to ask the Lord to give me the strength not to go backwards. Anya leaned in close and placed her lips on my neck then sucked on it hard. I jumped as my body tingled. "Mi still knowyuh spot dem." She whispered in my ear, switching her language on me like she did often when we dated. She eased over a little more and straddle me. Her ass felt so good in my lap. I gripped it with both hands as she continued to suck on my neck and unbutton my shirt. Her soft breast pressed against my chest and I closed my eyes thinking maybe I deserved to fuck someone else since Rose was fucking ole boy, but I just wasn't that type of stud. Two wrongs never made a right for me.

"Anya stop."

"Why?" She asked as she pulled my earlobe into her mouth.

"I can't."

"Yes you can," She leaned back and pulled her shirt over her head then unsnapped her bra. I asked the Lord for more strength. If I was a dude there would be rumors circulating right now that I was gay, because I wasn't taking full advantage of the pussy being thrown at me.

I lifted Anya up and carried her to her bedroom then dropped her on her bed. I pulled her pants from her body and she started playing with her box right in front of me. "Mineedyuh Snapps."

"Turn over you know I like that ass from the back."

She did as she was told. Her ass was stacked and I wanted to dig deep in her. I drew an invisible across from my forehead to chest like the Catholics would do. "Lay just like that, I'll be right back." I walked out of the room and grabbed her keys off the table then eased out of the door, because if I didn't leave, that girl was going to have me doing something I'd enjoy that moment and regret later. I'd returned her car in the morning.

CHAPTER 13

Snapps

I sat in my bed with an ice pack over my eye thinking about everything that had happened the night before. I wondered if I overreacted since I pretty much knew what I was getting myself into dating a chick that had never knew anything other than penetration from a real man. I had a conversation going on with myself inside my mind, reminding myself of the lie Rose told when she said she was happy with me, but then again she never really said she was completely lesbian. She never uttered those words. Shame on me was all I could think.

My mother walked into my room and handed me a plate of food. I was shocked that she didn't lecture me when I walked in the night before battered and bruised. She simply said, 'I can't control your life anymore, just make the right decisions for you,' then went to bed.

I grabbed my phone and clicked on my *Temper* app. I selected songs the pressed *Irresistible pain Featuring Patrice*. The song hit home for me. I told myself not to listen to songs that would only make me feel worse, but I couldn't help it. I bobbed my head to the music.*How did we get to this place in our lives*...was the first line

I picked up the fork on my plate and stuffed my mouth with eggs then grabbed a piece of smoked sausage and bit off of it. As I grabbed for my toast my door eased open and Rose peeked her head in. "Can we talk?"

"About what?" I bit my toast.

"Snapps I'm sorry."

"I bet."

"Really I am."

"Rose you're walking around with a damn baby in your stomach, when were you going to inform me?"

She hung her head, "I was going to tell you, I really didn't want you to find out that way."

"What way? Him preparing to inject more of his kids into you?"

"Snapps don't be an ass."

I laughed and shook my head. She was in her best friend's backseat with her ex and I wasn't supposed to be an ass? Yeah okay.

Rose walked over to the bed and sat down beside me. "Snapps I need you."

"You need me or a place to stay, better yet I guess you need a baby daddy now right, because I'm assuming since you're standing here you didn't miscarry? I can't help you there. I don't have a dick between my legs to be playing daddy."

"I could stay with Akeisha, I'll move out if you want me to just please don't shut me out. I'll give the baby up for adoption or abort it. I know what I did was beyond stupid and I'll spend the rest of my life making it up to you if I have too. I don't want to lose you too Snapps, please."

I cleaned off my plate and grabbed the glass of water that was on my nightstand. Rose moved closer.

"What's that on your neck?" She asked.

"Probably a passion mark."

"Where did it come from?"

"My ex."

"When the fuck did you see her?"

"You feel like you have the right to question me?" I looked at her from the side of my eyes and drank more water.

"You're right. I was just curious."

"If you must know I went over there just to clear my head, she tried to fuck me, I told her no then I got the fuck on out of there. Anything else?"

"Are you going to be a dick with me every day now?"

"I'm hurt Rose what the fuck do you want from me."

"Forgiveness and for you to tell me what to do."

"I love you Rose, I feel like I've loved you since I laid eyes on you, but man…"

Rose laid her head on my shoulder, "I love you too and I know that you love me, probably more than I deserve and I'm sorry. I feel so lost right now," her voice started to crack, "my mother is gone and shit just isn't the same. I don't know which way is up."

"I've been trying to show you which way it is, but you keep bringing yourself down, what the fuck is up with the cigarettes and I don't think I didn't smell the liquor on you last night."

"I know Snapps, I know. I need you to help me." She started to cry then wrapped her arms around me. I hated my emotions. I wanted to push her ass on the floor, but like a weak bitch I held her and rocked her back to a safe place. I had to be stupid. "We can fix this, I know we can." She whispered.

"Yeah, we can and I'm buying a gun."

"Why?"

"Because if I see your ex again I'm pushing led into homeboy." I meant exactly what I said.

Rose shook her head. "What about the baby? Do you want me to have an abortion?"

"I don't believe in those. I'll just pick up a second job or something I guess."

She nodded her head against my chest and wiped away her tears."So, are you going to pay for Akeisha's window?"

I ignored her question and finished cleaning my plate.

Akeisha

I blew smoke into the air as I waited on Rose to call me. I just knew Snapps would kick her out on her ass and I'd welcome her to the bottom of the food chain with open arms. I sat online in a chat room

132

while I waited. It had already been two hours since I dropped her off.

Ding! A private message had popped up.

StudSatisfaction101: *talk to me*
Femme4u:*Who are you?*
StudSatisfaction101: *If you talk to me you'll find out.*
Femme4u: *How old are you?*
StudSatisfaction101: *22 and u?*
Femme4u: *18*
StudSatisfaction101: *Mmmm young one*
Femme4u: *Only in number*
StudSatisfaction101: *So, what do you look like?*
Femme4u: *Don't you care what my name is?*
StudSatisfaction101: *Alright, what's your name and what do you look like?*
Femme4u: *lol it's Akeisha, I'm 5'4", chocolate, and thick and u?*
StudSatisfaction101: *I'm Vonya, but I just go by "Vee" and I'm better at showing than telling, go outwith me?*
Femme4u: *You might be crazy or something.*
StudSatisfaction101: *I'm not, but you're welcome to bring a friend, I'll bring one too.*
Femme4u: *Okay when and where?*
StudSatisfaction101: *Dinner? Tomorrow at seven?*
Femme4u: *what restaurant?*

StudSatisfaction101: *⬜your choice*
Femme4u: *hold on brb*

My cell phone lit up in my lap and I saw that it was Rose calling. I smiled as I thought of how hysterical she might be when I picked up, but to my surprise it was the opposite reaction as she delighted in the forgiveness she had received from Snapps. She went on and on about the long talk they had about "them". Snapps was a fucking idiot. I never understood why good people would hold onto bad ones, they couldn't be saved or changed. I frowned on the other line as she babbled about how good Snapps was and how she wasn't going to mess it up, but I knew better. I commenced my conversation with Ms. Satisfaction as she rambled on.

Femme4u: *So, what does your friend look like?*
StudSatisfaction101: *You tryna get at my friend?*
Femme4u: *Of course not. I want to see if she's my friend's type.*
StudSatisfaction101: *Oh we're playing cupid?*
Femme4u: *something like that.*
StudSatisfaction101: *You're friend won't be disappointed trust me. Pick a restaurant.*
Femme4u: *Applebees, I won't break you this time.*
StudSatisfaction101: *Alright the Veterans location cool with you?*
Femme4u: *Perfect.*

I logged off ending my conversation with Vonya. I knew there was no way in hell Rose would go out with me on somewhat of a double date since she was already in the hot seat, so I'd just have to make her believe it was a girls night or something. I was happy that Vee suggested the restaurant on

134

Veterans because it was a part of the city that Snapps was never in. Hearing Rose talk as if she was about to be a reformed sinner inside her relationship only fueled my plan more. I was determined to show Snapps that looks did not make a person good for you and Rose was definitely that bitch people were speaking of when they said everything that glitters isn't gold.

Snapps

Rose stepped into my bathroom to make a phone call. I stood by the bathroom door to see who she was calling and from the way the conversation started I could tell it was Akeisha. I needed to make a phone call of my own so I stepped away and dialed up Lexi.

"Speak ya peace." She answered clearly high as a kite.

"Nigga wassup?"

"Snaaappps," she drug out my name, "high as usual, what it do my nig."

"I need a favor."

"Anything I got you."

"I need a piece."

"Anything but that, what you need that for pretty boy, what you gon do with it?"

"Rose's ex dude knocked me in my shit last night and I just don't want him to think he'll be able to do that shit again. I just want to scare him."

"Scare him. I can handle that quick."

"No bodies Lexi." I laughed.

135

"Cool cool, but you know there are consequences with hot guns. If you do use it you don't know how many other bodies are attached to it and you'll have to get rid of it."

"You think I should buy one legally?"

"Highly recommend it. You can get away with so much shit with a registered gun. To me the only downfall is that you're weapon will always be able to be traced, but you ain't no major gang banger or no shit like that so I say do it the legal way. I could still handle that Emmitt character for you."

"No Lexi." I laughed again. "What you doing later?"

"Not a damn thing."

"Iight I'll come scoop you at around one so you can help me get one."

"Cool."

"Deuces."

Lexi and I hung up. Emmitt had better stay the fuck from around me and Rose and anything that had to do with Rose.

CHAPTER 14

Rose

I sat at the kitchen table eating a sandwich and attempting to look for a job in the newspaper. There was nothing appealing to me. I had never worked in my life and I was dreading the whole idea. The money that I did have left from my mother's policy and slowly dwindling down. Snapps and I had even sold everything from my mom's house but as I paid for clothes, shoes, and food for myself and tossed Snapps' mom a few dollars for bills that disappeared as well. I went ahead and paid for the rear driver's seat window that Snapps smashed on Akeisha's car too since it was mostly my fault that it happened. I guess her knocking on the glass would have been an under reaction with the state I was caught in, so I had to feel where she was coming from. I also figured that if I found a job we could move out faster. I was feeling uncomfortable in the house with her mom. She never complimented me or ever had anything nice to say to or about me at all. At first I just assumed it was that parental jealously that most parents had behind their children but as time went on it was obvious that it was something much deeper. Ms. Adams was mad ghetto and I never hesitated to show my disgust in how she was. She already hated me, so there was no reason for me to act as though I fancied her after everything that happened. Ms. Adams was a loud woman with tattoos all over. I had no idea how she held a job down at a hospital for so many years, looking and acting the way she did, but surprisingly people loved her everywhere she went.

Her eyes were always on me and I was going to lose it if she didn't stop looking at me out of the sides of her eyes. I did my best to respect my elders, but she was damn sure pushing it. I sipped on my juice then sat my glass back on the table, Ms. Anderson walked over to where I sat and lifted my glass, placing a coaster beneath it and slamming my glass back on the table. I chewed on my sandwich slowly and watched her as she walked over to the sink. She looked back at me and rolled her eyes. She turned on the water in the sink and started to wash the dishes. It was as if she was trying to annoy me and being ten weeks pregnant and emotional really didn't help me much. She tossed her dish towel in her water and swung around looking me in the face.

"Aren't you supposed to be on bed rest?" She inquired with a hint of attitude.

"I'm sitting down." I bit a piece of my sandwich.

"So just how pregnant are you?" She asked. I guessed it was kind of hard to tell just hard far along I was since I was barely showing.

"Excuse me?"

"You heard my question. I'm done tiptoeing around you and biting my tongue. How far along are you?"

I kept calm. "10 weeks."

She shook her head. "You ain'tno good."

I remained calm. "You may think so but Snapps thinks otherwise."

"Snapps is blinded and she thinks she's in love, but you see me, I'm not in love with you and I'll kick your ass all up and through this house. How could you do that to her?"

"I made a mistake."

"I've made plenty of mistakes in my life and none of them include accidental dick."

Before I said something that would get me back on Snapps' shit list I stood from the table, grabbed my sandwich and juice and walked upstairs to lock myself in the room. I picked up my phone and called Akeisha. It had been awhile since I talked to her because she had tricked me into going on a double date with some stud she met online, but thankfully they never showed up and it ended up just being us and some delicious food.

"Hey pregnant lady." She answered after two rings.

"Hey girl..." I said somberly.

"What's wrong?"

"Girl, Snapps' mother is about to make me choke slam her old ass in here. I mean she already makes it obvious that she hates my guts and just now I guess she decided to give me a little piece of her mind."

Akeisha laughed. "It's her daughter Rose. How are you going to feel if the child you carried for nine months comes home with a black eye because her girlfriend's ex boyfriend punched her and got her partner pregnant?"

"You make it sound so bad." I laughed.

"It is!"

"I'd rather her just ignore me. I'm starting to hate coming out of the room, because every time I do something she's reporting it to Snapps and she thinks I don't know."

"You want to come ride with me?"

"Please." I pouted as if she could see me. "I need to get out of this house."

"Alright I'm headed out right now I should be there in a few."

We hung up and I got up to put on some decent clothes and brush my hair, anywhere was sounding better than being in that house with Ms. Anderson at the moment. I couldn't deal with the tension. I needed to find a job or a hobby quickly since Snapps had picked up extra hours and was taking online courses for Computer Engineering. I almost never saw Snapps. She kissed me in the morning then eased into bed at night. She and I had not had sex since our incident, because as she put it 'the thought of Emmitt inside of me made her sick and turned her off.' She claimed that eventually she'd come around and I was hoping eventually would be soon, because this baby inside of me made me want to have sex more than ever and my hand couldn't keep doing the job.

Akeisha pulled up and blew her horn. I ran out of that house faster than a roadrunner to get away from Ms. Anderson before I hurt her. I hopped in the car and hugged Akeisha. "Thank you for saving me."

"You are so special." She laughed as she pulled off.

"Where we going?"

"Paint and Party."

"What's that?"

"What it sound like, paint and party girl. They provide the brushes and all that and we just bring drinks."

"How much is that?"

"Forty."

"Who's paying for that?"

"Girl my friend, now would you shut up."

I vented more of my frustrations to Akeisha as we rode to the event that I was unprepared for. I guess it was a good thing I couldn't drink so I'd definitely sit out for that part of the festivity. We pulled up and parked then we sat in the car and waited. "What are we waiting for?"

"Vonya and her friend."

"Not those same studs that stood you up."

"Vonya had an emergency, she apologized."

"You always find a way to drag me."

"I've never met her Rose. I just need reinforcement just in case she's insane."

"So, I'm guessing her friend is reinforcement too?"

"Yep."

"Yeah alright." I said not believing a word she said. We sat in the car for five more minutes until a

141

burgundy *Impala* pulled up beside us. Akeisha finally got out, but I sat in the car. She poked her head back in. "Get out heifer."

I rolled my eyes and eased out of the car, slamming the door behind me. Akeisha greeted her ugly online buddy, hugging her while I stood in the background. She turned and pointed at me. "This is my friend Rose and Rose this is Vonya," she looked her up and down and smiled that I want you smile as she ogled.

"Nice to meet you Rose," she reached out to shake my hand then tapped on her car window. All I could see was log curly hair as the other person stepped out. She turned around and my heart rate sped up and my eyes closed in her on light brown eyes and chocolate skin. "Damn," eased from my lips as I took all of her in. This was the first time that I had lusted behind another woman. I was attracted to Snapps, but so was everyone else because she was so damn fine. I fell for her more so for her personality than her obvious looks, but at this very moment this tall, smooth-skinned stud that was standing before me was making everything I felt for Snapps a lie.

"That's my dawg Blaze." Vonya said. Blaze walked around the car in her t-shirt and snug jeans that sagged just a little bit and I reached out my hands. She smiled and I damn near passed out from how beautiful she was.

"Rose." I introduced myself.

"I don't shake hands Rose." She smiled.

"Why not?"

"I prefer hugs," she grabbed my hand and pulled me into her chest and the cologne she wore

142

traveled graciously through my nose. She was nothing like Snapps who had taken forever to pursue me and tell me how she really felt. Blaze was forceful, confident, aggressive...I liked it.

Blaze and Vonya let Akeisha and I walkahead to the event. They provided the drinks and paid for our admission. We all settled in at an easel and pulled out paint brushes. Vonya and Akeisha sat in front of Blaze and I. I couldn't remember the last time someone made me sweat, but here I was nervous sitting beside Blaze as she watched me out of the corner of her eye and painted as the instructors helped us.

"You don't talk much huh?" Blaze asked.

"I actually talk a lot."

"Yeah? Say something then."

I chuckled. "I can't think of anything."

"Alright then I'll just poke around in your life then."

"That's fine by me."

"You have a girl?"

I wanted to lie, but I couldn't. "I do."

"I figured you did, you're too beautiful not to."

I blushed. "What about you?"

"Nope, rockin solo dolo."

"Nothing wrong with that."

"I guess not, but I do want one though."

"You probably have women lined up around the corner."

"That's what you think?"

"Yep."

Blaze pulled her phone from her pocket and placed it on my lap. "You hold on to that."

I laughed and finished painting. We talked a bit more. Blaze was nothing like I would have guessed from her looks. She was humble, laid back, and very blunt. She worked as a tech at car dealership and she lived alone. She was twenty-four and she drove a *Dodge Ram*. She had lost her parents in a fire and offered me words of comfort when I shared my lost with her, even if I couldn't have her the way that I wanted to, she was going to be a good friend to have since she empathized with my pain. I didn't want the day to be over, but I had to get back home eventually before Ms. Anderson called Snapps and put thoughts in her head since she didn't see who I left with.

Akeisha and Vonya shared a long inappropriate kiss behind Vonya's *Impala* that made me uncomfortable since Blaze was standing right there and I was sure she wanted to kiss me goodbye as much as I wanted to kiss her. I was never really one to rush things, but Blaze had the inside of me boiling. She hugged me tight for a long time then opened my door, kissed my cheek, and closed it behind me. Akeisha hopped in and started the car. The instant that they pulled off we both started squealing like teenage fan girls.

"Oh shit!" I looked at Blaze's phone in my hand.

"What?"

"She forgot her phone. Call Vonya."

Akeisha dialed Vonya, but there was no answer. "I'll just tell Vonya when she calls me back, let's get you home." Akeisha pulled off. We talked

144

about everything we learned about Vonya and Blaze as we rode back to the place I was calling home temporarily. I was fascinated.

Akeisha pulled up in front of the house and Ms. Anderson's car was gone. I was happy to have the house to myself for a couple of hours. I waved by to Akeisha then headed inside to shower. I went straight up the stairs and as I entered the bedroom Blaze's phone started to ring. I looked at it wondering if I should answer it then I decide against it and walked to pull out clothes so I could shower. The phone started to ring again and it was the same number. I told myself it could be an emergency and I answered.

"Hello?"

"So who has been calling me since you've had my phone?" Blazes voice serenaded me through the phone.

I smiled, "Nobody."

"Still think I have chicks lined up?"

"I guess I don't."

"Can you talk for a minute?"

"I can talk for two." I smiled and walked around still gathering things so I could hop in the tub.

"I think you should find a way to chill with me sometime this week."

"How am I supposed to do that?"

"That's what Akeisha is for right? I'd really like to spend some time with you."

"I have a girlfriend Blaze." I taunted her.

"We all have problems, so when can I come get you?"

I held the phone wishing I could just hang it up. I had a good thing going with Snapps, but another part of me needed desperately to explore these intense feelings for a stranger. I didn't want Snapps to be the only woman I dated if I was going to jump into this lifestyle and stay. I needed to try everything.

Snapps

I walked inside after another long shift. My mother was sitting up in the living room with a lamp on reading one of those cheesy romance novels that she loved so much. "Hey mama."

"Hey baby, long day?"

"Yeah as usual."

"I left your food in the microwave."

"Thanks." I turned to head for the kitchen.

"You know she was gone for hours again today."

"Mom don't start."

"You just need to open your eyes baby."

"They are open, she made a mistake, we…" Rose appeared at the top of the stairs as I was talking and I paused midsentence.

"Are you seriously explaining yourself about this situation again?" Rose said folding her arms across her chest.

"This conversation is between me and Sasha."

"Yeah well when I can hear it upstairs that makes me a part of it to. Why do you insist on talking about me? You that fucking miserable?" Rose said.

"Rose!" I yelled at her.

146

"Little girl please don't think because your carrying I won't get in your ass in here."

"You already made that threat earlier, quit talking shit and do it!" Rose became hysterical and so did my mother. I held my mother at the bottom of the stairs unsure when the tension built up this high. Rose moved to stepped down as she continued to yell back and forth with my mother. She attempted to rush down and before I could run up to stop her, she came tumbling down the stairs. Her back banged against the rail then she hit the floor hard landing face down. My mother stood with her hands over her mouth in shock.

"Sasha I didn't…"

"Call the ambulance!"

My mother rushed to grab her cell phone from the coffee table. Rose was out cold. I turned her over on her back and pulled up her shirt to check her stomach. I didn't think I'd care about that baby, but I did. I cried holding her in my arms until the ambulance got there. My mother and I followed in her car.

They pushed us to the waiting room once we got there. They asked a few questions about what happened then we sat and just waited. I looked over at my mom.

"It's not your fault." I reassured her, but she didn't say a word. "Mom…" I called out to her, "Mom…" I called out to her once more then she turned to look at me. "I'm moving out." I said and she still didn't say a word. She nodded her head in agreement and sat with her head down.

147

Three hours had passed then a doctor came out and spoke with us. I jumped up first.

"Hi, I'm Doctor Lucien," He reached out his hand and I shook it.

"I'm Sasha and this is my mother, is Rose okay?"

He smiled which gave me my answer before he could speak. "She's going to be just fine, but..." There it was. "She suffered a terrible miscarriage and has a mild concussion." The words stabbed me right in the stomach. My mother walked over to her chair and grabbed her purse and walked away.

"Can I see her?"

"Yeah, follow me."

The doctor escorted me to Rose's room and I wasn't ready to see the pain in her eyes for a second loss.

CHAPTER 15

Akeisha

I wanted to be heartbroken for Rose, but my own hatred had gotten the best of me as I thought to myself that's exactly what she gets. God knew that Snapps deserved better. She was already breaking her back to take care of Rose and she would have just killed herself trying to take care of a baby too. Rose claimed she was looking for work, but it seemed more to me she was just sitting around waiting on mommies money to run out. It was still a joke to me that her mother was in debt the way she used to look down her nose at me and drive around in her *Jaguar* that was repossessed after the funeral. Maybe it was the different men she had in and out that took care of her and made her think that she was more than she was and Rose was going down the same path only it would be dumb females taking care of her.

Vonya and I were hitting it off well since we met and from what I heard Blaze and Rose were hitting it off just as good between secret lunches and constant text and phone calls. This was just too easy. I really wanted to get Blaze alone and tell her the truth about Rose and just get her to play her, but I figured that would be no fun. Rose would do enough damage to herself and I'd be long gone when the shit started to hit the fan. My cell phone rang and I snapped out of my devious trance.

"Hey sweetie."

"Hey you, what you got going on?"

"Nothing, just waiting on my mom to get home, so she can cook."

"Why don't you cook?"

"I would, but I'm being lazy today. What you up to?"

"Nothing really, I was just thinking about you since I haven't heard from you all day."

"Aren't you sweet."

"How is your home-girl?"

"She's actually doing okay."

"You're a good friend you know that."

"I try my best." I sighed.

"Why the long sigh?"

"It just sucks being so loyal to someone who hurt you before."

"What you mean?"

"Nothing I don't want to bore you with our issues."

"I got nothing but time today baby tell me."

"Well you know the girl I told you Rose was dating?"

"Yeah"

"I actually liked her first, we even dated for awhile, but Rose went behind my back and fucked her."

150

"Damn like that? Why y'all still friends?"

"I guess I'm just a forgiving person. Sometimes I wish I wasn't."

"I'll have to tell Blaze to watch that one."

I smiled on the other end of the phone. "Nah don't do that, she really likes Blaze." I knew for a fact that Vonya would tell Blaze exactly what I said. It probably wouldn't turn Blaze completely off, but it would plant seeds of doubt in her mind and that would be all I needed once Snapps learned about them.

Snapps

The bell rang as one of the glass double doors to the station opened. I looked up from my register and saw my mom walking toward me. "Hey." I said.

"Hey," She said back almost in a whisper.

"What you doing all the way over here?"

"I came to give you something."

"What?"

She reached in her purse and pulled out a set of keys then handed them to me.

"What's this for?"

"I know you and Rose are looking for somewhere to live. I was going to give it to you after graduation when you established your career and I knew you could take on the responsibility, but it seems that you are ready to be more responsible than I give you credit for. It's the house your father and I purchased before he died…"

"I thought you sold it."

151

"He'd turn over in his grave if I would have given up that house just because he was killed."

A tear rolled down my cheek as I held the keys in my hand. "I know you're only nineteen, but you're so much like your father, making your own decisions even if they are bad." She laughed. "I can't keep holding onto you and after everything with Rose I see it's just time I let you be on your own since clearly age is not the defining factor of maturity." She took a breath "Did I mention the house is fully furnished?"

"Thank you mom," I walked around the counter and hugged her tight. I knew she felt guilty about Rose walking down those steps. She had been silent for days and so had Rose. They both blamed themselves and avoided each other, so moving out was definitely for the best.

She kissed my forehead then walked out of the store and I watched her pull off. My mind flashed back to my father. I still remembered his face. He and my mother were nothing alike. He was a college boy who wanted nothing more than to become a lawyer and take care of me and my mother. He got ran off the road by an 18-wheeler on his way home from taking the bar in another state. It was the state he wanted to live in. The phone call devastated my mother and she really hadn't dated anyone since. Instead she put all her energy into taking care of me and making sure she gave me the life my father wanted. She always told me stories about how much my father loved his black girl from the hood, my mom that is. I would sit and think to myself that if I found a woman I loved as much as my father loved my mother I would give her the world no matter what I had to do.

I looked down at the keys in my hand remembering the one story, three bedroom house they had just purchased before he was killed just in case he didn't pass the bar. He wanted to own different properties so when we traveled we'd never have to stay in a hotel. He also made renting the property out an option for extra income to be placed in my trust fund.

We had only been living there a week and everything had seemed to be perfect. I had made so many plans for my room. I didn't know if it was harder moving out of that house because my mother couldn't stand to be in the place or knowing that he had actually passed the bar after taking it three times and we'd never know what our new home was going to look like. I had never shared with Rose what happened to my father and now that I thought about it, she never asked either, but I couldn't wait to tell her.

Rose

I sat across the table sipping pink lemonade and munching on the spinach salad that I had ordered to be cute and not look greedy. Blaze sat in front of me staring me down.

"Aren't you going to eat?" I asked as my cell phone buzzed my seat.

"I'm not hungry."

"Then why did you ask me to lunch?" I smiled and pulled my phone from my purse to check my messages. *We're moving* read on my screen. I smirked a little then gave my attention back to Blaze.

"You said you were hungry and I'd use any excuse to see you."

I shook my head and continued to pick over my salad. Blaze and I had been hanging out whenever we got the chance, which was pretty often since Snapps was so occupied. I figured I should have been a bit more understanding since she was trying to make a life for us, but I wasn't so sure it was a life that I wanted. I thought maybe spending time with Blaze would help me to figure out exactly which direction I wanted to go in. I enjoyed her company and her conversation.

"You want to go out with me tonight?" Blaze asked.

"Where?"

"…just a gay club."

"They have those?"

She laughed. "Where do you think gay people hang out? I keep forgetting you're a newbie."

"Can I tell you something and be honest."

"You can tell me anything."

"I'm kind of afraid to say it because it might upset you or turn you off."

"Say it Rose, there isn't much I haven't heard."

"Okay…" I sat my fork down, "I still like men."

Blaze laughed again. "You thought that would be shocking?"

154

"Well, yeah."

"Sweetheart there are more 'lesbians' that fuck men than straight bitches."

"Wow."

"You have so much to learn. I expected you to still like men after you told me Snapps was your first and only girl. I'm just trying to find a way to convince you that you need to stay completely on this side." She grinned.

"Really…" I picked my fork back up and dangled it over my plate. "…so what's your master plan?"

Blaze adjusted herself in her seat, leaned forward, and licked her juicy lips. She placed her arms on the table and locked her hands together then looked into my eyes. She spoke in a low tone, "I'm going to show you everything that you've been missing. Your girl Snapps is a kid and I'm pretty sure that all she saw was skin and legs and she figured if she blew your mind with a decent nut, a bit of flattery, and attention then she'd get you on her team. Me? I'm a bit more complex than that. I see that you're beautiful and that's all good, but what else comes with that? I could see from the moment that I met you that you were empty in so many places. Being a lesbian is a lot more than pretty faces, clubs, and fucking. I'm not going to lay a finger on you. You are going to tell me exactly what you want and decide on your own if this is what you desire."

Blaze had my insides on fire no pun intended. I was so used to people laying themselves at my feet, but not her. She was so sure of herself and it was sexy. She was right about everything she said about

Snapps once I let her words sink into my brain. Perhaps Blaze was exactly what I needed, her maturity, her patience, her calm, her appeal, her knowledge of this life, her resistance to my beauty, and her certainty of herself.

I'd let her show me everything that she spoke of, but I'd hold onto Snapps in the meantime. I learned the hard way with Emmitt that every girl should have a backup.

We continued our conversation and Blaze continued to intrigue me. I sipped more of my lemonade then damn near choked when Emmitt walked in. He spotted me before I could hide my face and Blaze placed her hand on mine to make sure I was okay. I whispered, "Ex-boyfriend six o'clock."

Her head turned as she tried to see who exactly who he was. I smiled as he approached.

"Wassup Rose?"

"Nothing much, wassup with you?"

"…Just grabbing a bite to eat."

"When did you get back in town?"

"A few days ago, I had to come handle a few things. I'll be gone soon though. I don't have a reason to stay here." He said with obvious bitterness in his voice.

"I hear you, well, this is my friend Blaze."

"Emmitt," He grabbed her hand and shook it. "Looks like nobody can hold on to you huh? Where's your knight in shining armor Snapps?" He asked clearly being spiteful, but unaware that Blaze knew all about Snapps.

"She's at work," I said through clenched teeth, "And if I remember correctly you left me the first time."

"I tried to reconcile."

"Can we not do this right here, right now Emmitt?"

"You right my bad, I'm trippin, but can I get at you for a minute?"

I looked over at Blaze to be sure it was okay and she gave me the go ahead so I eased from the booth where we were seated and followed Emmitt off to the side. "What is it?"

"Yo, what happened to the baby?"

"I lost it…"

Emmitt stood shocked for a moment, then he shook his head and walked away without a word, leaving me to feel guilty as it if were me who killed our child. I walked back over to the booth and sat back down. "I'm sorry about that." I said to Blaze.

"It's okay, some people just can't take a hint. Now what was I saying?" She continued on and I finished listening.

Snapps

"Where you going looking all good?" I watched Rose walk back and forth, dressing and putting make-up on.

"Just…out with Akeisha."

I let out a huge sigh. "I don't trust you with that girl."

"You don't trust me with anyone."

157

"True, but this is different."

"Uh huh, hand me my shoes."

I picked up Rose's heel. "Can I have a kiss first?"

Rose turned and looked at me. "You want to kiss me?"

"Yeah, why wouldn't I?"

"Well I mean since you know…"

"Why did you have to remind me?"

"I'm sorry."

I handed Rose her shoes and left the room. I was just starting to get the images of her and Emmitt out of my head and she had to go and ruin it buy bringing it up again. I was sick all over. I sat in the living room and switched on the television. Rose walked in with her heels on and hovered over me. "I'm really sorry Snapps."

"Okay have fun." I said as I pretended to watch television. Rose kissed my cheek then left.

$\mathcal{R}ose$

"You are a bold bitch you know that?" Akeisha said as I buckled my seatbelt.

"How?"

"Gay clubs are tell-all venues. All it will take is the wrong person to see you with Blaze in there and it will get right back to Snapps."

"Nobody knows me."

"Okay, I won't protest." Akeisha sped off.

Blaze and Vonya were standing out front waiting for Akeisha and I when we walked up. Blaze

158

pulled me into a tight embrace and inhaled my perfume. "You look nice." She smiled, "and you smell nice to."

"Thank you." I smiled back at her as she grabbed my hand and pulled me into the entrance. Blaze paid for us both then we headed upstairs toward the music. Neon lights were all over. The bar was lined with people talking and laughing and almost everyone had a drink in their hand. Studs stared at me as I walked in, biting their lips and pulling down their shades. Some femmes looked too, smiling at me while others whispered to their friends. There was nothing I hated more than a hating as bitch. I swung my hair and held my head high to give them all that *yeah bitch I look better than you* look. I was not easily intimidated.

"You want a drink?" Blaze yelled over the music.

"Yes please!" I yelled back.

"You'll be okay over here by yourself for a minute?"

I nodded my head and she stepped to the bar. I looked around at my surroundings. I couldn't believe I was standing in a club filled with gay women and men. It was quite comical to see the gay men acting more like the women and the studs standing around like men. I watched Akeisha as she hugged different people and danced like she was a regular, which I didn't doubt she was. Blaze returned with my drink and stood behind me bobbing her head to the music. I wanted to wrap her arms around me. I wanted people to think I was hers. I was so attracted to her it was a shame and the way she kept her distance made me

159

feel rejected which only made me want her that much more, Akeisha brought several people over to me to meet me. I just smiled and nodded until a slow song came on.

Blaze meant what she said about not laying a finger on me aside from the hug she had given me earlier, but I wanted her to touch me. I grabbed her hand and tossed my empty cup in the nearest trash receptacle. It was apparent that everything was going to have to be my call. I figured if I gave her an opening she'd just run with it, but she didn't as I pulled her to the dance floor. I grabbed her hands and placed them around my waist then pulled myself into her. Blaze grinned as I moved my hips side to side. She leaned and whispered into my ear. "You better stop it. This is not what you want young lady."

"You don't know what I want."

"Do you?"

"I want you."

"Are you sure about that?"

"I was sure at lunch."

"You better take that back."

"What if I don't want to?"

Blaze placed both hands on my ass and squeezed tight then pushed her lips on mine. Her aggression made me soak my panties. I was definitely going to have to trash those before I went home.

The song switched to this stud *Country G's Drop That featuring RKhane300Million* and got hype. After Lexi told me about stud rappers I went on a search and had been hooked ever since.

I danced a bit more then decided I needed to pause for a drink. Blaze offered to go and get me bottled water, but I needed to walk so I headed for the bar. I squeezed through the crowd almost perfectly until a shoulder bumped me hard. I turned to see who it was that couldn't say excuse me. "I know you see me trying to get through." I said as I turned around and laid eyes on Snapps' ex Anya.

She smiled. "If a nuhlikkle miss browning"

"Wrong country bitch."

"If I wasn't on probation I'd bust you over the head with this bottle bitch, in plain English."

I raised my hand in the air to swat the spit from Anya's mouth but Akeisha and Blaze walked over before the situation could escalate. Anya backed off laughing then yelled over the music. "Tell Snapps hello!" She winked and walked away.

I danced on Blaze all night. It was nice to be around someone who didn't know my past and didn't really care about it. It was just nice to get some positive attention.

CHAPTER 16

Snapps

Rose and I stuffed our things into the backseat and trunk of my car. Akeisha volunteered to tote whatever wouldn't fit into my vehicle. I had not realized Rose had so many clothes and shoes until we started boxing things up. I didn't complain though since all we had to pack was clothing. I could imagine how hectic it would be if we had to move furniture too. Since my mother had the house furnished I wouldn't have to buy anything new for a few years, which would give me a chance to save money and keep paying for school.

My mother stood in the doorway as we stuffed the last of our things into Akeisha's car. I walked over to her and handed her my copy of the key, but she pushed my hand back. "Keep it. Come over anytime you want."

"Mom I'm going to be ten minutes away." I laughed because she was acting like I was moving to another state. I hugged her and kissed her cheek then

I walked over to the car so we could head over to our new place.

We pulled up and I smiled as I thought about my dad. I hopped out of the car and stood on the sidewalk just staring at the house I was supposed to grow up in. My mother used to complain about it being all white, but I loved it. I would swing around the blue poles out front and my dad would sit watching me. I didn't have many memories here, but the ones that I did have put me in a place of solace. I pulled the keys from my pocket and walked up the pathway to the door to open it. It had been years since I set foot in that house. My mother and I would drive by it often, but we would never go in. Akeisha and Rose started pulling bags from the car as I walked in to look around. The smell of fresh paint and new carpet approached my nose. I loved the smell of anything new.

Akeisha and Rose walked in behind me. "Where is the main bedroom?" Rose asked with bags in her hand.

"First room around that corner." I spoke over my shoulder and pointed then headed back out to the car to grab some boxes.

Akeisha and Rose goofed around and put away clothes while I unloaded the rest of the stuff from the car. I shook my head and laughed because somehow I knew I end up having to do all the hard labor while they sucked up the cool air. I carried another box into our bedroom and dropped it on the floor. "Could y'all at least go pick up something to eat if you aren't going to do anything?"

164

"Hey, we're working hard in here." Rose smiled. "I'll go grab us something though, what are you in the mood for?"

"Tacos"

"You always want tacos." She laughed and grabbed my keys that dangled from my right pocket then kissed me on the cheek.

"Don't you need some money?"

"No baby I got it." she said as she headed out of the door. I shrugged my shoulders then plopped down on the living room sofa. I heard Akeisha's heavy feet against our tile and rolled my eyes as she entered the room and sat on the love seat beside the sofa.

"So how are you Snapps?"

"I'm good."

"I didn't ask you how you looked."

"Really?We using old sugar daddy lines now?"

Akeisha laughed. "I was just paying you a compliment."

"Tell me something Akeisha."

"Anything."

"How do you manage to smile in Rose's face and try to fuck with me behind her back?"

"The same way you manage not to tell her. I think you like it."

"You have life and bullshit messed up if you think you flatter me at all."

"You are so sexy when you're mad."

"I think you should go."

Akeisha stood up slowly. "I'll go but I'll be back. You'll come around one day Snapps, remember who wanted you first."

I shook my head as she headed for the door. The moment she was gone I stood up to do some organizing. I made a list in my mind of the things I needed to buy like dishes and towels. I was really grateful that my mom had furnished the place for me and all I had to do was get the simple stuff. I headed to the bedroom and lay across the bed staring at the ceiling. I started to imagine the life Rose and I could have together in this home. The life my mother and father never got to live. I was going to give her everything.

The door eased open and Rose walked in with my food. "Five hard shell Taco Supremes and a large Raspberry Tea." Rose stood at the end of the bed. "Where's Akeisha?"

"She had something to do and where'd you get money from?"

"I still have a little left from the policy. I've been spending carefully."

I looked over at the closet with all of her things. "You sure about that?" Rose popped my leg and handed me my food. She pulled out a gar and plastic bag with weed in it. "You've been smoking that stuff so much that you've learned how to roll it?"

"At least it's not cigarettes." Rose slit the gar open pulling out the tobacco inside and replacing it with the weed she had broken down. It was sexy yet disturbing as I watched her tuck, lick, and roll. A part of me loved the innocent Rose that I met with a broken heart, but the other part of me had a soft spot for this new, tainted Rose who wanted nothing more than to escape the recent misfortunate events of her life. Rose pulled a lighter from her pocket and ran the flame across the blunt then set fire to the end. She put it up to her lips and inhaled. "Try some…"

I didn't protest. I just pulled it from her fingers and hit it twice. I had never told Rose that I smoked when I was in middle school until my mother beat me to my next birthday. A lot of the things I did had a lot to do with the women I was attracted to. I passed the blunt back to Rose then stuffed my Taco into my mouth. "So who started you with smoking weed?"

"Akeisha"

"I should have known."

"Why'd you say it like that?"

"Man that girl is bad news."

"You've been saying that forever."

"That's because it's true."

"You don't even know her."

"You should say that in a mirror."

"She's been my friend since seventh grade."

"Years don't make someone your friend."

"I don't want to argue about this."

"Who's arguing?" I snatched the blunt from her fingers and hit it two more times. I finished off my tacos then hopped out of bed to change my shirt and put on shoes.

"Where are you going?" Rose asked.

"Gun range with Lexi."

"When did you buy a gun?"

"Does that matter?" Rose folded her arms and sat Indian style in the bed as I dressed. "I'll see you later."

"Later when?"

"I don't know. Lexi and I are going to play pool after we leave the range and I might catch a game or two."

"What am I supposed to do all day?"

I laughed. "Call your *friend* Akeisha."

Rose rolled her eyes and I headed out.

Rose

I stretched out across the bed smiling. I was happy to be out of Snapps' mothers' house. I could now walk around freely without hearing snide remarks or having her over my shoulder reporting my every move. I walked through the house thinking of every way I could decorate our new residence.

DING! DONG!

I stopped in my footsteps wondering who that could be when no one knew where we lived. I walked to the front and looked through the peephole. "Shit," I said to myself when I saw Blaze standing on the other side. I opened the door and poked my head out. "What are you doing here?" I whispered as if someone could hear me.

"I heard you moved into a new place and I wanted to see it."

"Who told you that?"

"Akeisha who else; can I come in?"

"No."

"Why not? Your girl isn't here. Her car would be parked out front."

"I guess Akeisha told you what kind of car she drives too?"

"You guessed right, now invite me in."

I moved back and opened the door to let Blaze in. "You can't stay long."

"Alright I won't stay long. You need to relax."

"I am relaxed." I stood with my arms folded. "What are you doing here Blaze?"

"I wanted to see you."

"You couldn't call first?"

"I wanted to surprise you."

I laughed. "I'm surprised now tell me what you really want."

"I'm trying to figure out why you're playing this game. One night you're tonguing me down in the club and the next you're playing house."

"I can't just leave."

"Why not?"

"It's complicated." I put my head down.

Blazed leaned back against the wall. "I get it, you feel sorry for the baby stud."

"Not exactly."

"That's what it is. I'm cool with that. I'm very patient so I'll let your lil relationship run its course. Call me when it convenient for you." Blaze walked toward me and pulled me into her, brushing her lips against mine as though she was going to kiss me, but instead she kissed my cheek then walked out of the front door. I locked the door behind her and smiled touching my lips. Blaze was something serious and she did something to me that I couldn't explain.

169

Snapps

"Seven corner pocket." I leaned over the pool table to place the ball in its promised destination.

"You always gotta show off pretty boy." Lexi said as she pulled on her cigarette and walked around the pool table. "I need to tell you something…" Lexi said in a low tone.

"What is it?"

"You know I'm not the gossiping type."

"You're not the beat around the bush type either so what is it?"

"I saw your girl in the gay club dancing with some stud."

I stood up and held my pool stick beside me. "What were they doing?"

"Just dancing from what I could see."

"Oh well I'm not going to trip off that man."

"I just thought you should know."

"Good looking out homie." I smiled. "Now go find us a bitch of age to get us some drinks while I finish beating that ass."

"I'll do you one better since I'm smashing the bartender." Lexi winked and walked off.

I concentrated on the ball, playing it cool when on the inside I was dying to know who Rose was dancing on in the club and if dancing was all they did. I kept telling myself that I trusted her and our past was our past but my instincts wouldn't settle.

CHAPTER 17

Rose

Snapps and I had been in our new place for over two months. I stood in the mirror looking at myself in my uniform making sure that I was flawless before my shift. I had found a way to have my cake and eat it too. Blaze mentioned to me that they were opening at her job for service writers and cashiers so on one of her off days I went and applied and they hired me on the spot. She was surprised to see me on my first day and I was just flat out happy to see her.

I had come to the conclusion that what I felt for Blaze was pure lust and infatuation and Snapps was the one that I loved. I wanted them both. I needed to make Snapps trust me and I wanted to make Blaze fuck me.

Snapps and I were having sex again, but the things we did were limited. I had to play the role with Snapps as if all the attraction I had for men was gone, so I protested whenever she wanted to use a strap on me. I hated that I had to pretend, but something in me was afraid to lose her and to lose all that I gained being with her. I wanted to be selfish for a little while. After all that I had been through I felt that I deserved it. "Baby I'm dressed!" I yelled from the bathroom.

"Well come on then."

I switched off the light and grabbed my purse then headed to the kitchen where Snapps was seated eating a big bowl of *Captain Crunch*. "Why didn't you make me a bowl?"

"You didn't ask me to."

"Always thinking about yourself, get up so we can go."

"Now you want to rush me after you spent two hours in the bathroom."

"It takes work to look this good."

Snapps shoved as much cereal into her mouth as she could then hopped up and grabbed her keys. I followed her out of the door and locked it behind us.

I pecked Snapps on the lips and hopped out the car so I wouldn't be late clocking in. Blaze was standing by the clocking waiting to clock in as well when I walked in. "Nobody should look that good in a uniform."

"I could say the same thing to you."

"You're running kind of late this morning, you usually beat me here."

"Snapps was having breakfast."

"You need your own car."

"I can't afford one right now."

"What if I let you drive my other car?"

"What would I tell Snapps?"

"Baby you work at an auto shop, tell her it's a loner."

172

"You're seriously going to give me your car?"

"Yeah why not? I can't drive two."

I smiled then hugged Blaze tight. "What time do you get off tonight?"

"8:30"

"Okay I'll call Akeisha and tell her not to pick me up. I'll just ride home with you to pick it up."

Unruly customer after unruly customer came in as the day went on. I watched Blaze as she did her thing. I was sure it was pretty obvious that there was something between us by the way we smiled and stared at each other every time that we worked together. I couldn't say a word to her without the corners of my mouth curling up.

I called Akeisha on my lunch break to let her know that she didn't have to pick me up. Blaze was sitting in her truck when 8:30 rolled around, waiting for me to join her. I had to close out my drawer and turn in all my receipts before I could go, so she was usually done before me. I hopped into the car with her and we headed to her apartment. "I just realized that I've never been to your place."

"You would have been by now if you were mine."

"Don't start."

"I'm not."

We pulled up to her gate and she pressed in a code to get us inside. We parked and then headed into her apartment. She flipped on the light and it was just as I thought it would be. She had a flat screen hanging on her wall, one sofa and it was barely decorated. "This place could use a femme touch."

"Move in then." She laughed. "You want something to drink?"

"No I'm good." I sat down on her sofa as she headed to the kitchen. She came back with a bottle of water and leaned against the wall. "Aren't you going to sit down?"

"No, I think I'll keep my distance."

"Can't resist me?"

"No, I need to shower. I've been under cars all day." She laughed.

"Let's go shower then."

"You want to shower with me?"

"Yeah, I do."

"I think you want something else."

"Why would you say that?"

"Do we really have to play this game?" Blaze sat her bottle down and looked me dead in the eyes. She unbuttoned the top of her uniform never breaking her stare. She slid off her shoes then pushed her uniform down to the floor. She pulled the t-shirt that she wore beneath it over her head, leaving her in nothing but a sports bra and boxers as she pulled off her socks. I swallowed back hard thinking I just may have bitten off more than I could chew. Blaze was going to destroy me. I could tell from the way that she looked at me that I wasn't getting into the ring with an amateur. I couldn't let her see me sweat though.

"Are we going to shower now or what?" I pulled the hair tie I had around my wrist off and pulled my hair up off my neck.

"Follow me." She said. I stood and walked slowly behind Blaze as her bare feet pressed into her tan carpet. She led me into the bathroom and didn't

174

bother to turn on the light as she closed the door behind us and I leaned against it waiting for my eyes to adjust to the darkness. She walked over to the shower and switched it on. The water seemed louder without my sight. I stood close to the door. "Don't get scared now." Blaze's voice echoed off the walls.

Scared was an understatement as I shivered against the door where she couldn't see me. I heard Blaze drop something to the floor. I assumed it was the rest of her clothes. She walked over to me and confirmed that she was naked as she grabbed for my wrist and pulled my hand up to her chest. I gasped surprised by her touch. Her breasts were just big enough to fit into the palm of my hands as I ran my fingers across her hard nipple. I swallowed back hard as she pushed my hand down between her legs. That was the first time I had placed my hand on a pussy that wasn't mine. Snapps never let me touch her there. I never assumed she didn't want me touching her and until she gave me the go-ahead I was going to keep my hands to myself. Blaze on the other hand knew exactly what she wanted and wasn't shy about it and I liked that. "Am I going to have to undress you?" Blaze asked standing close to my face. I didn't say a word as Blaze felt all over me then plucked the buttons on my shirt a loose one by one. She pulled it from my body and not too long after everything else followed. She stepped back and the sound of the shower curtain hooks rang in my ears. "Get in." She said as she guided me and I did as I was told. She eased in behind me wrapping her arms around me and sucking down on my neck. The combination of the warm water and her warm mouth had me tingling all over. She squeezed both of my breasts and nibbled on my skin. All I could think was that Snapps had never made me feel that way. Blaze eased her right hand down my body and paused between my legs pressing her middle finger against my pearl. My head flew back involuntarily as she massaged in circles. I pushed my hand against the shower tile and my fingers traces the lines as I struggled to hold myself up. Blaze wrapped one arm around my neck, holding me up as she split my lips to come inside of me. Her fingers glided in with ease. She slithered in and out until I came. I moaned so loudly it was embarrassing. I bent over beneath the water not sure if I had ever cum before with Snapps or Emmitt. I took deep breaths. "You alright?" She asked and I nodded my head yes. I stood back up and she began washing my body with only a bar of soap. I closed my eyes and let the feeling linger. I didn't want it to ever end.

We both stepped out of the shower and Blaze flipped on the light then dried my skin with a towel then herself. I wrapped the towel around me and picked my things up from the floor. I walked into Blaze's room to dress myself, but she had other plans as she took my clothes from my hands and tossed them back on the floor. "Blaze I…" She pushed her tongue into my mouth before I could get out another word. I fell back onto the bed and she pushed my legs open and moved down to be face to face with my lady. I wasn't ready for what was coming as she wrapped her lips around my lady. I almost suffocated her as my thighs locked around her head. It was obvious that she had been doing this a lot longer than Snapps as she licked my pussy from the bottom to the top. She flipped me over sucking on my pussy from behind. It felt so good I wanted to slap her. I pulled the sheets from her bed and looked for more things to dig my nails into. Blaze held nothing back as she inserted two fingers into my from behind and pushed me down onto the bed so that my stomach touched the mattress. My mouth was dry as I screamed out her name and cussed loudly. I was getting what I had been craving and then some as Blazed fucked me into a new era. She flipped me all over her bed and sucked on every part of my body. The way she ravished me said one thing: it had been a long time since she fucked someone and the way she made me feel I was glad that I was the first in awhile. Blaze held me down on the bed as a new sensation stronger than the one before arose in my body. My eyes watered and my toes curled. I couldn't contain myself. I screamed out as I tried to relax my muscles to enjoy the intense feeling then I released and dropped. I looked over at Blaze, "What was that?" I said out of breath.

Blaze smiled, "you just had your first orgasm."

"How you figure it was my first?"

"You wouldn't have asked." She winked and kissed my cheek.

I laid still a little bit longer then I showered again and dressed so I could beat Snapps home and pretend to be asleep.

"I wish you could stay."

"I know. Me too." I said then kissed Blaze goodnight. She closed the door to the *Camry* she was letting me borrow and waved. I pulled off and headed home.

I pulled up and parked on the right side of the driveway then went inside to shower. I undressed at the door and walked straight to the bathroom. I turned on the shower waiting for the water to warm up then I stepped in. I smiled as I let the water hit me. My vivid imagination took over and I remembered the touch of Blaze's hands and her soft lips. I bit down on my lips as I grabbed my towel to wash between my legs.

CHAPTER 18

Snapps

My alarm went off at six in the morning as usual. I rolled over and Rose wasn't in bed. I pushed myself up and rolled out of bed then went into the bathroom to brush my teeth. I wasn't really in the mood for work. I wasn't in the mood for anything. I just felt thrown off. I splashed water in my face to wake myself up then I headed into my closet to pull out my uniform.

Once I was fully dressed I walked into the kitchen and Rose was standing with a huge smile on her face and two plates of food on the table. "You cooked?"

"Yeah come sit down and eat."

"Hell no, you trying to kill me."

"No, I'm not. Now sit down."

"I didn't even know you could cook."

"There's a lot you don't know about me Snapps."

"Obviously," I pulled out a chair and sat down. I picked up my fork and tasted the eggs first

179

and they were actually good. I grabbed the syrup that she already had sitting in the table and poured some over my pancakes. I sliced them with my fork and closed my eyes because they were filled with butter and were fluffy. "Your mom taught you how to cook?" I asked with a mouth full of food.

"The one and only."

"Go moms." I said as I stuffed more food into my mouth. "You need to start cooking every day."

"Maybe I will."

"I'm looking forward to it." I said as I stuffed my last piece of food in my mouth then washed it down with orange juice.

Rose stood up and removed my plate. "So what time are you getting off tonight?" She asked.

"Seven, why?" I asked suspiciously since she never cared about my schedule before.

"Just wanted to know what time to have dinner ready?"

"You're off today?" I asked curious since I knew she had to work.

"Yea, but I'll be home before you, so I'll cook tonight."

"Alright cool." I said then stood from the table and walked over and kissed her lips. Her kiss didn't feel the same. I backed away slowly then headed out of the door.

I still had a lazy feeling and didn't want to go to work or do much of anything so I when I got into my car I called Lexi. It took her forever to answer.

"Why you calling me so early fool?"

"I need somewhere to chill until Rose goes to work."

"Nigga why you dodging your girl?"

"I just want a day to myself man. I'm exhausted and I don't want to go by my mom."

"You know you welcome to come over here."

"Okay then I'm on my way." I hung up and pulled off.

Rose

I called Blaze the instant Snapps was out the door. "Hey beautiful." She answered.

"Hey you, what are you doing?"

"Thinking about you."

"Funny I was doing the same thing. I've actually been thinking about you all night."

"Is that right?"

"Yeah and I had an idea."

"What you got?"

"Why don't you call in today and come spend the day with me."

"Don't you have to work today toomiss?"

"They won't miss us." I smiled where she couldn't see me.

"Alright I'm down. Let me shower and I'll be there in a few."

"Don't make me wait. Come shower here, I'll wash your back."

"Okay I'm sold. I'm going get in my truck right now."

We hung up and I finished cleaning the kitchen. Blaze had done something to my body and I wanted to feel it again. I dried my hands and walked

181

back toward my bedroom and had another thought. I called Blaze back. "You need me to bring something?" She answered.

"You must be reading my mind."

"What is it baby?"

"I want you to use a toy on me."

"Oh so this is a morning booty call." She laughed.

"Well you didn't think we were going to sit around watching television or something did you?"

"I didn't think that at all."

"So are you going to bring a toy or what?"

"Yeah I got something for you." She chuckled and we hung up again. My pussy was throbbing just from the thoughts of Blaze and what she could do.

I needed to kill time until Blaze got there. She had turned me into an addict overnight. I called Akeisha because I needed to tell somebody.

"It's almost eight in the morning tramp you better be dying."

"I had sex with Blaze." I could hear Akeisha shifting fast.

"What?"

"Yep, last night and oh my gawd it was soooo good! I can't think about anything else."

"You are so nasty." Akeisha laughed.

"Kei you don't understand. That girl's mouth is magical. I had my first orgasm."

"Damn. Okay so what about Snapps? Are you going to leave her?"

"No! I love Snapps. I just want to fuck Blaze until I can't fuck her no more."

"I thought you had feelings for Blaze."

"I mean I do, but not like I do for Snapps. Snapps has been there for me."

"Blaze could be there too if you let her."

"You're probably right. It would just be too hard to choose."

"I hear you pimpstress." She laughed.

"Shut up." I said as the door bell rang. "I have to go Blaze is here."

"Bye tramp." Akeisha said then hung up.

Akeisha

I smiled as I hung up the phone with Rose. Since she didn't know how to choose I was going to help her. Today was the moment of truth. I called Snapps cell phone the instant I hung up. I was going to tell her Rose was cheating without telling her. I needed to pick her brain first to see exactly what I could say to get her home.

"What Akeisha?"

"Damn why you have to be so rude. You haven't had any coffee yet?"

"I don't drink that shit, now what do you want?"

"I was calling to see if I could come pick up your key to get in your house. I left something over there the day I helped y'all move and I need it."

"Hell no you can't have my key. Why didn't you call Rose?"

I smacked my lips, "She didn't answer her phone so I'm guessing she at work already. Can you just meet me over there or something? It doesn't have to be right now. It can be on your lunch break."

"Actually I'm playing hooky today."

"Does Rose know that?"

"No, and I would appreciate if you kept your big mouth shut."

"You're secrets safe with me."

"What you left at my house anyway?"

I had to lie quick, "My driver's license. Rose said she put it in her drawer for me."

"You've been driving around without a license all this time?"

"The police don't bother me."

"Fine whatever. I was about to go play ball anyway. I'll pass by the house to see if it's there and drop it to you after I'm done balling with Lexi."

"Okay cool and tell Lexi fine ass I saidwassup."

"Girl you want everybody." Snapps laughed and hung up the phone in my face, which was fine with me. My mission was accomplished.

Snapps

I watched through my bedroom door as another stud fucked my woman. The woman I had lived to love for the last three years. Yes, I've done my dirt, because I'm not a perfect nigga, but what the fuck had I done to deserve this? Rose has always been everything in my eyes, but right now as this other stud smashed her from behind, she was just some bitch to me. People think that just knowing you were

184

cheated on hurts, but to me that's just your mind playing tricks on you. Actually seeing the shit with your own two eyes is where the real pain lies, because the picture is drawn for you. I could see she didn't give a fuck about me each time her mouth opened to let out a sound of wanting more of someone else inside of her. I could see that she had no respect for me at all as she rocked that she and I slept in every night and woke up in every morning.

How long had this shit been going on? It was taking everything in me not to get the burner out of my car and put a bullet in both of their pussies. I felt tears forming in my eyes as I watched and listened to this other bitch pleasing what belonged to me. Rose never even let me hit her with a strap, but here she was on her hands and knees, taking that shit like a fucking soldier. I thought back to everything in my mind that should have brought on suspicion, but the love I had for her kept fanning it away. My hands started to shake so I excused myself hoping that maybe I could I calm myself down. I made a deal with myself that I would take a ride and when I came back if the car I didn't recognize was out of my driveway I'd leave, but if it wasn't I wouldn't be responsible for what happened after that.

I walked out the door and got back into my ride, so that I could think clearly. I called Akeisha. The bitch had to know something if not everything and I wanted to know it all.

"Hello." Akeisha answered on the first ring and I was sure it was due to the fact that she *had* to know something.

"Akeisha?"

"Snapps?"

"Yea."

"Did you find my license?"

"No but I have a question for you."

"And what is that?"

"Can I swing by?"

"What you can't ask over the phone?"

"Look bitch, I'm over the whole I-don't-know-nothing acting-like-I'm-dumb game alright? I'm on my way over, don't question me." I ended the call fuming with anger.

I pulled up in Akeisha's driveway and she stood outside waiting on me. I knew she was going to want something so I prepared myself. It was nothing to pump her head up and make her think she's about to get something that she wasn't.

"You didn't have to be so damn rude on the phone." She licked her lips at me and I damn near gagged.

"I'ma just get straight to the point. Is Rose fucking over me?"

"Why you asking me that?"

"Because you're her best friend and I know you know!"

"I am that and even if she was, why would I tell you?"

I moved close to Akeisha, "Because I got something you want."

"Is that right," she grinned. "Finally coming around just like I said you would." Akeisha rubbed my arm. But I pushed her away.

"Info first…"

"No kiss me first."

186

Somebody just kill me now I thought to myself as she puckered her lips and leaned toward me. I pecked her lips just enough not to feel sick and for her to believe she just might get a chance after all the bullshit transpired.

She leaned back "Mmm you've been drinking strawberry soda."

I held in my laughter as she licked her lips. She was disgusting. "Okay, now tell me."

"Alright," she switched into the living room and I followed. "She pulled a blunt from her table, placed it between her lips and lit it. "Aren't you going to sit down?"

"No, I just need a quick synopsis."

"Okay, okay, her name is Blaze."

"The stud?"

"Yeah."

"Where'd she meet her?"

"Online or something."

I remained calm. "How long she been talking to her?"

"I don't know four maybe five months I think."

"Man you fucking lying."

"Am I?" She hit her blunt and blew smoke. "She's in your bed right now right?"

"How the fuck do you know that?"

"You think this is the first time she done been all up and through your shit?"

I balled my fist at my sides. "What else?"

"The car Rose is driving is for Blaze and if you don't believe me just check the glove compartment. Blaze's real name is Leticia Monroe."

I looked away, squinting my eyes, thinking about the "loaner" lie she told me.

"You're too cute to be so naïve. I thought you would have at least known they worked together."

I swung my head back around. "What?!"

Akeisha laughed and shook her head. "You work too hard."

I punched Akeisha's wall and ran out of her house to my car as she yelled out my name. I sped to my mother's house and let myself in. She heard the front door slam and ran down the steps. "Sasha?" I ignored her call and went straight to the shed behind our house to retrieve the gas can that I knew she kept half full. I walked back into the house and past my mother to the junk drawer to pull out a box of matches. "Sasha what's wrong with you?"

"I need a good lawyer." I said as I walked out of the front door, slamming it behind me and hopped back into my vehicle. My skin was hot and I was shaking. I was on a mission. How dare that bitch play me like that after everything that I had done for her? I had a taste for vengeance and the flavor was Rose. I wasn't sure if my hatred was geared more toward the fact that she lied or the fact that she downright disrespected me in my parent's house. My cell phone rung constantly and I kept sending it to voicemail. I already knew that it was my mom. I'd explain myself to her later.

I pulled up in front of my door and a single tear fell from my right eye. I looked over at my driveway and the *Dodge* was still there. I deemed myself irresponsible from that point on. I pulled the blunt I started smoking that morning from my ashtray

188

and put it to my lips then dug through my CD's. I pulled out one that I had burned awhile back and pushed it into my CD player. I switched the track 12. *Irresistible Pain by Temper* vibrated through my ears giving Rose and her bitch approximately two minutes and sixteen seconds of fantasy lane before I busted it up and brought them back to reality. I had never felt the kind of pain I was feeling in my body that I felt at that moment. I kept my blunt in my mouth hoping it would save me from myself as I puffed on it, hoping possibly/maybe it would calm me down. I got out of my car and walked behind it then popped my trunk with my keys and placed them in my pocket. I grabbed the hammer and gas can that was back there and walked over to the *Camry* she had been parading around in for months as if it were a perk of her job. I smashed the window to the passenger side and thought to myself that I had busted one too many car windows being with this bitch. I opened the glove compartment to check the name on the registration and sure enough just like Akeisha said, it read Leticia Monroe. I threw the papers onto the passenger seat and poured gasoline over the car then I walked over to the *Dodge* and did the exact same thing. I know I had no reason to burn up the truck, but the way I was feeling anybody could get a taste of my wrath. Either she knew about me and just didn't give a fuck enough to respect my mind and the pussy that belonged to me or she was just in the wrong place at the wrong time. Either way I didn't give three fucks as I pulled the matches from my pocket and struck one then tossed it on the car and walked away.

The flames didn't draw them out of the house, but how could it when they were probably still in there fucking. I dropped everything back into my trunk then walked back to the driver's side and pulled my gun from under my driver's seat. It was still somewhat illegal for me to have a gun since I couldn't get a license for a hand gun until I was twenty-one but at that point I was willing to take my chances with the boys in blue where my emotions were involved. I blew the horn until the front door finally swung open. I spoke out loud to myself, "Look who finally decided to look out the motherfucking window."

Blaze ran outside and I ran around my car. She came at me and I hit her in the face with the butt of my gun. It knocked her out instantly. Rose finally made it to the front with a sheet wrapped around her body as I drug Blaze into the house. "Surprised to see me?"

"Snapps what the fuck are you doing?!"

I dropped Blaze behind the door seal then shot her in both legs just in case she woke up and wanted to play super-save-a-hoe.

Rose ran, slamming and locking the door behind her. I stepped over her Blaze's body and walked toward the door. I could hear her screaming and crying from the other side. I banged on the door with the end of my gun, but got no response. I was getting more pissed by the second. I hit the door harder, but Rose refused to open it. I knew I didn't have much time because my nosey ass neighbors were probably beginning to come outside by now. "You should really study law Rose, it's quite interesting!" I yelled through the door. "Did you know that if you shoot someone inside your home you won't get convicted?" I banged on the door again. "ROSE OPEN THE FUCKING DOOR!"

She screamed louder from the other side. I never stopped to think twice about what I was doing. Her and her little bitch could spend forever together in the fucking hospital.

Since Rose refused to let me in, I shot the lock and opened the door myself. It was my fucking house. Rose ran to the bathroom inside our bedroom. BAD IDEA! I ran behind her and punched her in the back of the head. I tucked my gun in the back of my pants and then kicked Rose as hard as I could. She grunted from the pain and tears continued to run down her face as she begged for mercy.

"Snapps please, don't hurt me."

"Hurt you? Ain't that about a bitch!"

"Why Snapps, why are you doing this?" She cried an ugly cry.

I kicked her again. "Bitch I gave you everything. I was there when nobody else was and you wanna know why?" I kicked her again, "was she worth it Rose?" I kneeled down, turning her over and straddling her and wrapping my hands around her neck, "huh, was she?!" I squeezed tighter choking her. "ANSWER ME!"

Tears began running down my face. I was really starting to feel the pain now. Rose looked into my eyes and all I saw was fear. Images of everything that had ever happened between us, the good and the bad, replayed in mind, but only temporarily. The image of Rose moaning and enjoying the sex of another stud drowned out our memories and I couldn't take it. I came down on Rose's face hard with my fist, almost breaking her jaw. I kept hitting her until I saw blood. I stood and pulled her up by her neck, because my anger was now bitterness, bluster, rage… The same rage that had busted a window, doused two cars in gasoline, and pulled the trigger a few minutes ago. I held my hands around her neck as she struggled to breathe. She tried prying my hands from around her throat, but she wasn't strong enough. Her life was slipping away and fast.

I couldn't do it. I couldn't kill her. I let go of Rose and she hit the floor. I ran outside and hopped into my ride and I was just in time as fire trucks and police cars weren't too far away. The sirens got louder and they got closer.

I sped off and I had no idea where I was going. I just needed to drive. I beat on my steering wheel as I cried and cussed at myself. I didn't know how to feel. I just knew that I was hurt, so hurt that I had shed blood and thought to take a life that I had no right to. I played God. I needed somebody to pay for this heartache. Every turn that I made led me right back to where I started. I pulled up to Akeisha's house and the door was still unlocked from when I left the first time. I yelled through the house as I stepped in.

"Akeisha! Where the fuck you at?"

"Snapps?"

She came running her husky ass to the front of the house like she was really worried about me. She reached for me asking what happened when she saw the blood on my clothes, but I slapped her hands away.

"You did this bitch! You knew she was fucking over me and you never said anything. You probably encouraged it, you sloppy bitch!"

"Snapps calm down."

"No fuck that! Fuck you!" I screamed hysterically.

I charged at Akeisha and slammed her up against the wall. I wanted to hit her so bad, but I didn't. I knew it wasn't her fault. I needed and wanted to take my rage out on anyone. I fell down on the floor and cried like a bitch. Akeisha tried comforting me, even after I flipped out on her. I jumped up and left again. I had to get away. I had officially lost my fucking mind. I decided to check into a hotel and try to calm myself down for the night. I knew this was bound to get worse before it got better.

Rose

"This one's alive", echoed in the background of my mind as my head pounded and my eyes fluttered open. I saw a face hovering over my body, but everything was still a blur. The lips were moving on the face, but I couldn't make out the words. I felt my body being lifted from the floor and placed on a cushion. I couldn't move. This was not my life. How could this be happening to me? Everything on my body ached, but the one thing that was filled with the most pain was my heart. I brought this on myself, bringing another stud into my bed. I had never seen

Snapps that way. She should have killed me. I wondered where she was now. I had no right to even be concerned, but I was. Tears fell from my eyes as the EMT's worked on my bloody and swollen face and my hearing started to come back slowly. They pushed me into the back of the ambulance and the bright light over my head hurt my eyes. I wanted my mother.

The ride seemed long as my body shook with the moving ambulance truck. I was dazed as they pumped drugs into my system to keep me stabilized.

Once I finally got to the hospital the doctor's and nurse's patched me up and stuck me in a private room. I sat in that bed just staring at the walls. My life was a complete mess and I had no idea how to clean it up. Snapps was nowhere to be found and Blaze was surely paralyzed. My thoughts got deeper and then they were interrupted by a knock.

"Come in." I said with swollen lips and a sore throat.

"Ms. Anderson there are some detectives here and they want to ask you a few questions."

I didn't say anything. I just watched the door widen as a man and a woman walked in. I wasn't in the mood for this shit, but I knew I needed to co-operate.

"Ms. Anderson I'm detective Ryan King and this is my partner Shelby Stone. You might remember us from your mother case."

"I remember…"

"We need to ask you a few questions and you would be well advised to answer truthfully and to the best of your ability."

"Yea, sure."

"First, we need you to tell us exactly what happened."

My eyes watered as I thought about Snapps and the look in her eyes. She didn't say two words to me or to Blaze. She just pulled out her gun and knocked Blaze cold then shot her like it was second nature her. That wasn't the Snapps I knew. Everything was fresh in my brain, but I refused to talk, so I didn't. "I don't remember."

"Ms. Anderson you do understand that this is can be an attempted murder charge and if you withhold pertinent information you two could serve serious prison time. I understand that this may be difficult for you, but we need to know what you saw."

"I don't remember."

"Alright Ms. Anderson I get it. I'm going to give you my card and when you're ready to talk give me a call." Detective Stone said as she left her card on the stand beside me and left my room.

I was all fucked up. I couldn't figure out what had gone wrong. How could Snapps have known? What was it that could have made her so angry? Nothing came to mind. I reached for the phone next to my bed to call Akeisha. She was all I had right now and I needed her. I dialed her number but she didn't answer.

This was my fault. I didn't think it would come to this.

****Snapps****

FUCK! FUCK! FUCK! FUCK!

I had to calm down. I pulled into the parking lot of a cheesy motel, making sure to park toward the back. I tossed my gun in the trunk and then I walked toward the front to pay for a room, so that I could get myself together. There was a little foreign lady sitting at the front desk. She stared at me, waiting for me to speak.

"How much for the night."

"35.99 plus tax."

"I'll take it."

"You pay with cash?"

"Yea."

I gave the little Indian looking lady forty dollars and snatched the key from the desk. I knew this place was as low budget as they got, she didn't even ask for ID. I went straight to my room and turned on the television. I'm sure my face was all over the news by now. My legs wouldn't stop shaking as I waited for something to pop up on the fuzzy screen. It took about ten minutes for the screen to clear up. Just as the television cleared, the News Anchor was flashing off and my house flashed on the screen behind a little Asian lady.

"Here in a local suburban area only moments ago it was reported that gun shots were fired and local residents smelled smoke. Emergency vehicles arrived to find Leticia Monroe with two gunshot wounds in her legs and another female

*identified as Rose Anderson brutally beaten. Police
are in search of the owner of the home Sasha
Adams who was said to have been spotted fleeing the
scene before Police arrived. Neighbors say that
Adams and Anderson were quiet residents and never
usually had company up until a few months ago
when the vehicle you see torched behind me showed
up. Rose Anderson is in the hospital in good
condition. No information has been released on
Leticia Monroe. The Police are searching for more
witnesses, back to you Karen.*"

They rambled on about the story for a few
more minutes and then it was on to the next. I sat at
the end of the worn down bed with my hands under
my chin. I heard everything that the reporter said, but
MONTHS stuck out to me the most and it didn't help
my frustration. I felt myself getting angry all over
again. I had a lot of unanswered questions and the
only person who could answer them was Rose.

I dozed off in my trifling ass room when I
heard a hard knock at the door. My heart pounded a
mile a minute in my chest. All I could think was that I
was found. I heard the little Indian lady from the
opposite side of the door and I was instantly relieved.
She was just doing her rounds. She said a few words,
none of which I understood, then I shut my door.

I checked my cell phone in my pocket and I
had a missed call from Akeisha. What the fuck did
her fat ass want? I wasn't sure if I wanted to call her
back. She might be trying to set me up, but then again
if she wanted to turn me in she would have done it
already. I decided I'd call her back, because I knew

197

that she had probably been in contact with Rose. The phone rang once and Akeisha picked up.

"Snapps! Where are you? Police are all over searching for your ass."

"I think I know that Akeisha."

"Why did you just leave like that?"

"Um I don't know, maybe because I shot somebody! What the fuck do you want?"

"I want to help you."

"Help me what?"

"Getaway."

"And go where Akeisha? I'm not running."

"So you're going to turn yourself in?"

"Yea, but not until I talk to Rose."

"She don'twanna talk to you."

"Bitch, did I ask you that?"

"Snapps you gon stop talking to me like that!"

"Or what? What the fuck you gon do? I already shot one motherfucker today. I don't mind adding you to the list. Find a way for me to talk to Rose."

"How? She got cops surrounding her ass."

"Bitch you kept the fact that she was fucking another stud behind my back for months to yourself, I'm sure you can manage a fucking phone call."

"Fine."

I hung up the phone and decided I needed to take a shower. I had a few things in my car, so I went out to get them so I could wash my ass. I made sure that there were no police in the area, because those bitches had my exact description from a photo they took from my house.

I stood in the shower allowing the water to run down from the top of my head to my toes. I was starting to think that talking to Rose probably wasn't a good idea. There was nothing that she could say to me to ease my pain. She used me. I had set all my dreams aside to make sure she was okay and this was how she repaid me. I hated to admit it to myself, but my mother had been right about everything she said about her and now I was in a situation where my freedom was at risk. I wasn't worried about them trying to prosecute me for bitch ass Blaze since she was trespassing, but beating Rose would definitely get me a domestic violence charge.

I stepped out of the shower and shook my dreads. I felt clean but that shower did nothing for my nerves at all. I sat at the end of the bed just gazing at the television. I could feel myself starting to daydream, but my phone snapped me out of my trance. I looked over at the night stand to see it lighting up. I walked over to check who it was. It was my mother. I took a deep breath and answered. "Hello"

"Sasha?" She screamed.

"Yes mama."

"What did you do? Why is your fucking face all over the news?!"

My mom didn't let me get a word in. She just tore into my ass, all the hood in her that she tried to mask with education came out as she cussed me from A to Z. I guess you can say I got my attitude honest. I've heard about my mama stabbing niggas, busting windshields, and stalking her old boyfriend's new bitches just for GP up until she met my dad and he

made a conservative woman out of her. My mama
was off the wall for real. "Mama…" I attempted to
cut her off.

"Is this about that girl? I never liked that bitch.
I told you that from day one. She looked like trouble.
All those pretty little young girls are nothing but
fucking trouble. If you would have listened…"

"Mama…"

"If I were you, I would have killed that bitch.
You better tell me what happened, before I get really
upset, because the news is making you look like some
type of monster, an armed and danegerous criminal. I
didn't give birth to no damn criminal…"

"MAMA!"

"What girl? You better have a good reason to
be constantly calling me and interrupting me!"

"I'm trying to tell you what happened, but you
just keep running your mouth."

"Are you disrespecting me right now? I know
you're not playing with me. I'll find your ass before
the police does and prison will be the least of your
worries. You understand me?"

"Yes ma'am."

"Now tell me everything."

I ran the whole story down to my mama. I
even started crying, because it had just hit me how
much I was really hurting behind the fact that Rose
played me all the way to the fucking left. I had no
idea how to feel. I was pissed, hurt, and still wanting
to hurt someone. I wanted everyone to hurt because I
was hurting. My mom tried to ease my mind a little,
but her words only calmed me temporarily.

After talking to my mom I fell back on the bed and dozed off without realizing it. I woke up in the middle of the night in a cold sweat. The images of Blaze and Rose had settled in a permanent place in my mind, taunting me, making me happy that I had reacted the way that I did. I didn't deserve what she did.

CHAPTER 19

Rose

Snapps was all that I could think about. Most would say that I was a stupid bitch for what I did and they would come down on me for missing her right now. I know, the nerve of me right? I just wanted to hear her voice and tell her everything. I wish I had known that she would lose it, because now Blaze was somewhere wondering if she'll ever walk again I was lying in a hospital bed, half way dead on the inside and lonely. Akeisha still hadn't called.

I wanted to call Snapps' mother, but that woman hated me and I'm sure if anyone had talked to Snapps, she had. She never spoke to me when we went over to her house after we moved out and even after the stair incident she still under-eyed me. She gave me dirty looks and right about now, I could only imagine what she wanted to do to me. I was safer right there in that hospital bed, than anywhere that that woman could get to me. I must have thought about her too much, because just as I was about to sit up and call a nurse, Ms. Adams walked in.

"Mrs. Adams what are you doing here?"

"Surprised?"

"Kind of, no, how did you find me?"

"I do work in a hospital."

I hung my head low at my own stupidity and prepared myself for whatever was about to come next. I knew this wasn't one of those friendly 'how are you' visits.

"Why did you do it Rose?"

"Do what?"

"Oh, now you want to play stupid. You know exactly what I'm talking about."

"Ms. Adams I honestly don't have an answer for you."

"You better find one. My baby is about to go to prison because of your trifling ass. You know, I never had a problem with her lifestyle. I never cared who or what she did until the day she brought you home."

Ms. Adams walked closer to my bed, making sure that I heard every word that she said. She pointed her finger directly at my face, tightening her mouth, trying to restrain her festering anger.

"There was always something about you, too beautiful for your own fucking good! You had Sasha blind, but you never fooled me. I was exactly like you once, young, beautiful, and careless, but there is also something that separates us."

"And what's that? I'm classy and you're just some ghetto trash?"

Ms. Adams slapped me and grabbed me by my throat, slightly cutting off my air supply and lifting me from the bed. She hovered so close; I could feel her breath on my nose.

"No you little bitch. I have respect for the people who dared to love me. Sasha loved you and what did you do? You took it for granted."she released my neck, letting my head fall on my pillows. "I've instructed Snapps not to speak with you. It's sad that after all you did to her she still wanted to talk to you, but that's not going to happen, because those days of minding my own business are long gone. We'll see you in court." She shot me a look that would have killed me and started for the door. Before walking out she mumbled 'she should have killed you' and the door closed.

The tears fell fast as soon as the door was shut. I wasn't crying because I was hurt or for Blaze or Snapps, but because Ms. Adams was right. I took Snapps for granted. I underestimated the love she had for me. How could I? When did I become this person? I held my hand to my throat, and then thought about my mom and tear after tear fell down each cheek.

Snapps

BOOM BOOMBOOMBOOM
I jumped up fast. My heart was going a mile a minute. I didn't want to answer. It could be the police. *What to do? What to do?* That's the only thing that was going through my mind as I panted and pushed shit around the room.

"Sasha open this damn door!"
"Ma!"
"Yes, now open up!"

205

I opened the door and grabbed onto my mom for dear life. It could have been housekeeping; I would have hugged them too. I was just happy to see that it wasn't the police, coming to drag me out, kicking and screaming.

"Girl get off of me. I'm bringing you to turn yourself in."

"What? Mama I was going."

"When?"

I just looked at her. I had no idea when I was going to go. I had enough money saved up to stay in that motel for another ten years at least. I should have never told my mama where I was.

"Come on. Put your shoes on. The longer you wait, the worse you'll make it on yourself. You created this mess and now you have to face the consequences of your actions. I raised you better, hiding in hotels and shit. Bring your ass."

I gave my mom everything that I had with me except for my driver's license because I was sure they were going to lock me up. I wanted to cry, but I had done enough of that and I was also afraid that my mama would back hand me for being a pussy about the situation. I wasn't that sure she would though, because I could see the hurt in her eyes as we pulled up slowly in front of the police station. I stepped out of the car after we were parked, taking a deep breath. My mama came around to my side and grabbed my hand. I felt like a kid again as she said 'come on baby, let's get this over with.'

I walked up to the front counter and told the cop who I was. His head popped up and he told me to stay right where I was. I had become a local celebrity obviously. I stood at the counter and waited then the officer returned and asked me to follow him. He instructed my mother to have a seat and she did as she was told. I followed the cop to an isolated room. He told me to have a seat then offered me water or coffee. I didn't want either. I just wanted them to book me already.

I sat in that room for what seemed like an eternity staring at the ugly walls with absolutely nothing on them. It was like a torture chamber minus the whips and chains. The door finally opened and in walked Detective Shelby from Rose's mom's case. She held out her hand to me, "I don't think we've officially met."

"You're detective Shelby."

"That's right and you are?"

"Sasha, Sasha Adams." I started to sweat.

Detective Shelby took a seat in front of me and pulled out a tape recorder and sat in on the table between us. She locked her fingers in front of her and leaned forward into my face then spoke, "Look I'm not going to bullshit with you Sasha. There isn't a damn thing that I can do to you right now. You've left me at a dead end because one I can't get Rose to admit you beat the living crap out of her or that you shot Leticia and two Leticia is still in the hospital in a coma." She leaned back. "This is what I'll do. I'll press play on this recorder and you can give me a full confession and walk out of here with a simple battery charge and vandalism or you can keep your mouth shut, get a lawyer which will make mommy out there go broke, and do at least twelve to fifteen."

I leaned back in my chair laughing on the inside. What Detective Shelby didn't know about me was that I wasn't stupid. The moment I purchased a gun and felt that I'd have to use it one day I began studying law; I had even thought about taking it up as a major. The property belonged to me and by law Blaze and Rose were both trespassing. She could probably stick vandalism on me for the cars, but at the most I get a slap on the wrist and community service since all of this was first offense, with the right judge nothing would happen to me being that love was involved. I'd plead temporary insanity and pretend to forget everything that I did. Hearing that neither Rose nor Blaze had said a word I had a plan. "I'm not saying a word without my lawyer."

Detective Shelby clenched her jaw and picked the record up from the table. She wanted me to tell on myself too bad, but I was smarter than that. She told me I was free to go and I damn near ran back out to my mom. She stood and held on to me for dear life. "Are you okay?" She checked me from head to toe.

"I'm okay, let's get out of here." I drug my mother from the station and to her car. "Give me my phone." I reached out my hand to my mother and she dug through her purse to retrieve it. She placed it in my hands and I called my job first to let them know I'd be out for awhile. My co-worker promised to cover for me as much as she could. I knew that crush she had on me was going to come handy one day.

"I got you a good lawyer baby."

"Good because I'm going to need one."

My mother drove me to my house. It was still surrounded by yellow police tape. I pulled it all down

208

and let myself in. I just needed to grab a few things. I walked into my bedroom slowly still disgusted by the smell of sex I was sure I was making up in my own head. The sheets and covers were still messed up and the pillows were on the floor. I hope that bitch got a good nut because it was probably her last for awhile. The part of me that felt guilty about all that I did refused to exist as I stood in that place where Rose broke my heart for the second time, first time shame on her, but second time shame on me because I let it happen again. I tried to shake the thoughts and do what I went to do and that was get a few things to wear. I packed two bags then headed back out to the car with my mom.

Once I made it to my mom's place I showered and lay back in my bed to think of my plan. The first thing I was going to do was stick myself in somebody's therapy sessions. If I was going to plead insanity I had to prove that I really had blacked out. My mom had already had a long conversation with the lawyer she had for me and told him everything that I told her. He was talking some shit about crimes of passion, which I was cool with if it would play a part in my freedom. My cell phone rang loudly as I moved on to the next step in my head. I looked at the I.D. and it was Akeisha. My first thought was to not answer it, but then I remembered that I told her to get Rose to call me. I hoped it wasn't Rose though. My mother and lawyer had advised me not to speak with her since she could probably record our conversations and at that point I wasn't putting anything past her grimy ass. I picked up with an attitude. "What is it?"

"Snapps it's Akeisha."

"No shit, I can read. What you want?"

"Rose wants me to ask you something."

"The answer is no."

"You didn't even let me ask."

"Do I really need to?"

"Look she's being released from the hospital today and she wants to know if she can stay in the house."

"For what she wants to bask in the ambience of Blaze's memory in my bed?" I said sarcastically.

"No, Snapps."

"Yeah whatever she can stay there, I'm staying at my mom's anyway. If I was a cold-hearted bitch like her I'd let her sleep on the street." I crossed my ankles. "Why can't she stay with you?"

"She doesn't want to face Vonya."

"Who the fuck is Vonya?"

"Blaze's best friend, my girl friend, she's been staying with me and my mom."

"Hold up…You fucking the best friend?"

"Look Snapps I have to go the nurse's are calling me." Akeisha hung up.

I held the phone in my hand just looking at it. It had suddenly dawned on me that everything was a set-up from jump, because I could have sworn Akeisha told me Rose met Blaze online. I know damn well they weren't doubling dating on chat. My skin was hot again like it had been for the past few days. Everybody was playing me for a fucking fool.

I was so happy to finally be leaving the hospital, but also sad because I'd be going back to the house where everything in my life fell completely apart. Everything was still a bit blurry to me. I understood fully what went on, but I wasn't exactly sure why it went down the way that it did. I was sure Snapps was at work that day and had no reason at all to be home. The missing piece to the puzzle was the only thing that had me anxious to get back to the scene of the somewhat crime. I wanted and needed to get past this.

The nurse handed me my discharge papers then finally began wheeling me to the elevator so we could get down to the first floor. I hate the whole wheelchair process. Snapps had knocked me in the face. My legs were perfectly fine.

Akeisha was at the front entrance waiting for me. She held a vase with twelve dozen roses in it. I smiled at the sight of her familiar face. "You don't answer the phone for two days but you show up to pick me up." I shook my head and Akeisha opened her car door for me. I stood from the wheelchair and got into Akeisha's car the pull the door shut. I leaned my head back against the seat and exhaled.

Akeisha hopped in on the other side. "How you feeling?"

"My head hurts like hell, but other than that I'm fine."

"That's not what I'm asking." She said as she finally pulled off.

"You mean Blaze and Snapps?"

"Yeah…"

"I don't have any words really. I just keep seeing Blaze lying on the floor and that painful look in Snapps eyes," I rubbed my hands across the vase, "I don't know how I let it get this bad."

"Rose, I need to tell you something."

"Oh boy I hate when people say that."

Akeisha inhaled then exhaled. There was a long pause before she spoke and I just waited."I kind of told Snapps about Blaze."

I stared at the flowers before me, hoping that my ears were playing tricks on me.

"Rose…"

"I heard you!" I yelled. "Why would you do that Akeisha?"

"I had so many reasons." Akeisha said in a voice of plea.

"Reasons? Reason's like what?!"

"You know I liked Snapps first!"

I throw the vase at Akeisha as she drove and we swerved from side to side. She tossed the vase to the back and was covered in water. "Are you trying to fucking kill us?!"

"Pull the fuck over!" Akeisha pulled to the side of the road and I hopped out needing a moment to breathe. Tears fell from my eyes as I grew more furious. "Balze is in the hospital and prison is waiting for Snapps! How could you do this?!"

"I didn't know Snapps was going to react the way she did."

"You really are fucking stupid! I should have listened to my mother and Snapps! Everything they said about you was the truth! How can you call yourself my friend?"

"How can you call yourself mine when you fucked Snapps!"

"That was high school!" I was frantic now and all I had was my words to cut deep into Akeisha and I was going to use them well. "She never fucking wanted you! Have you looked at yourself? You're fucking disgusting! On top of being nothing to look at, you're a horrible person!" Akeisha punched me in the face and I fell back on the ground. I refused to let her get the best of me this time. I looked around on the ground for something to hit her with. I was done with this bitch. My life was ruined now because of her. Of course what I did wasn't great, but she didn't even give me an opportunity to be honest with Blaze or Snapps or myself for that matter. I found a thick branch as Akeisha charged at me. I waited for her to get close enough and swatted her over the face with it. Her hands flew up covers the spot where I had gashed her. I kicked her hard and she hit the ground. I stood and ran around to the driver's side of the car and sped off leaving her on the side of the road. I saw her cell phone in the middle console and backed up on the street and tossed it out the window. The friendship I thought we had was over.

Snapps

I needed to relieve some stress. I looked over at my closet then stood from my bed and walked over to it opening the door. I had two straps at the top wrapped in plastic inside of shoeboxes and on the inside of each lid was the name of the girl I used it on. I pulled out the one for Anya and put it on then pulled my jeans over it and called Anya.

"Wassup car thief." She answered.

"You busy."

"Not exactly."

"What's not exactly, either you are or you're not."

"I'm not if you have something better for me to do."

"I got something for you to do."

"The door will be unlocked."

I hung up the phone and eased down the steps so my mother wouldn't question me. I grabbed her car keys and tiptoed out of the door. I hopped into my mother's car and sped off before she could recognize it was her engine revving and start blowing up my phone.

I pulled up to Anya's and the front door was unlocked just like she said. I welcomed myself in and when I swung the door open the smelled of burning incents filled my nose. Anya greeted me with nothing but a t-shirt, a shot of *Patron*, and a thong. I looked her up and down then tossed back my shot. She grabbed my hand, pulling me over to the sofa where I voluntarily sat down to let her rest her ass in my lap.

"Funny how you always come to me to run away." She said she straddled me and leaned into me with her arms around my neck.

"Who says I'm running away?"

"I bet Rose doesn't know you're here."

I ran my hand up Anya's thigh to her back, then over her breast and up her neck before stopping behind her head and merging my fingers with wads of her hair and snatching her head back. It wasn't usually like me to be rough because I was more of a sensual person who chose to take my time, but the sound of Rose's name had awakened my aggression. "Rose who?" I said as I pushed her head forward and sucked her lips into my mouth. I went there for one reason and that was to fuck her until I felt like myself again or at least partly. Although Anya sucked as a girlfriend she had always been good at what she could do with her pussy and mouth and I was about to take full advantage. I pulled the front of her shirt down stretching it around the collar and ripping it a little so her breast would fall out.

Anya placed a free hand near my zipper and pushed down on the strap that bulked my jeans then pushed herself up with her knees to grind on me. I freed her hair to place both hands on her ass cheeks and squeeze them like stress balls. I loved how soft her skin was and the thickness of her flesh between my fingers. "I missed pulling these dreads." She whispered into my ear.

It was déjà-vu as I lifted her from the sofa and carried her to her bedroom, tossing her on her bed and flipping her over, and pulled her ass up into the air. I grabbed her pussy from behind and the juices damped my hand through her thong. I pulled them from her body the removed my jeans to free my strap. Anya's ass looked like as apple so I leaned down and bit into it, slithering my tongue all over it. I smacked it as I stood back up then grabbed my strap like it was my real life dick and rammed it into her pussy. She moaned loudly as I pushed it in as deep as I could get it and held onto her hips. It was flesh against flesh as her ass smacked against me and I showed no mercy and no TLC to her pussy. My dreads bounced against my back and sweat dripped down my face. Anya screamed fuck me into the air over and over and that's exactly what I did.

"Let me ride you baby." Anya begged, but I ignored her. I was running the show tonight. I stopped and pulled Anya from the bed by her ankles, making her bend over and stand on her feet. I didn't give her time to maintain her balance as I reentered her and slammed against her once more. Her nails scratched her sheets and her moans grew louder with every hard thrust forward. I leaned down and grabbed her wrist, pulling her arms back as if she was being arrested and thrashed her. I just wanted her to take it all anyway that I gave it to her.

I decided to give her a break and let her lie on her back. I pushed her legs up over my shoulders and slid into her, stroking her slow, but hard and watching as her breast bounced up and then down again on her chest. Anya reached for me, she squirmed beneath me, she squealed. I felt powerful as I held her legs up and controlled when she would feel pleasure. This was exactly the feeling that I needed since my life was out of control.

"Make me cum Snapps." She moaned I tingled all over.

I started to stroke her fast again. I dropped one leg and placed my thumb over her clit to enhance whatever it was that she was feeling as I took

216

advantage of her body. Anya started to shiver and I knew that meant she was about to explode. This would just be the first one. I had a lot more stress to relieve. It was Anya's lucky night.

CHAPTER 20

Snapps

I turned over in the bed aching, but feeling more alive than I had in awhile. It had been a minute since I stayed up sexing all night; I mean in-between work and studying I didn't really have the time to. Rose and I would get it in as much as we could but most of my free time was spent sleeping. I turned over on the animal print sheets that Anya had on her bed and yawned. I needed to get up, brush my teeth, and put my freedom plan into motion. Anya was already out of bed. I eased out not really wanting to move. I tried to remember when I got ass naked then I just shrugged it off because whenever me and Anya fucked anything was bound to happen. I searched for my boxers and sports bras then I heard a throat clear. "Looking for these?" Anya bit her bottom lip. She walked over to me slowly to hand me my boxers. "You have somewhere to be?"

"Yeah, I have some business I need to tend to."

"You mind me asking what?"
"Why you so interested?"

"No reason, I just wanted us to spend the day together."

"Where's your ex-bitch?"

"Not here."

I shook my head, "What you got in your fridge?"

"Anything you want. I went to the store while you slept."

I finished dressing then I walked past Anya and into the kitchen. I pulled juice from her fridge and drank it straight from the jug. I turned to look over her counter at the television and started to choke on the juice already down my throat when Blaze's picture flashed on the screen. Anya ran to the front when she heard me choking to see if I was okay. I moved her out of my way and walked toward the television to turn it up.

"Twenty-four year old Leticia Monroe was pronounced dead this morning around 6:30am when her charge nurse went in for a routine check and found her unresponsive. The doctors are saying that Monroe suffocated in her sleep, but they have not yet released the how or why…"

I tuned the television out thanking God for being on my side. I didn't wish death on Blaze even after what happened, but now that she had passed the only other witness was Rose. I jumped up and grabbed the keys to my mother's car. I needed to talk to Rose. My mother would just have to be upset with me for awhile.

Rose

My eyes barely opened as the sun started to beam in through the blinds on the back glass sliding door that led to the patio. I turned over on the sofa and pulled the cover over my face. I had cried all night thinking about how I got here. I had hurt Snapps and Blaze. I found out after all that Akeisha was never my real friend. I hated myself for always defending her when all along she was just stabbing me. I wanted this to be a bad dream. I wanted my mother to walk in and pinch me then hug and kiss me. Nobody in the world had this much bad shit happen to them so quickly.

I turned over on the sofa, pushing my face into the back pillow hoping to smother myself, but the doorbell rang. I hate the dreadful sound of that damn doorbell. I sat up and looked in the direction of the door wondering who the hell could be bothering me while I was trying to be depressed in peace. I stood up and wrapped the cover around myself and drug it with me to the front door. I walked across the floor cringing at the memories of the blood I had just scrubbed up a few hours ago. "Who is it?!" I yelled but nobody answered me. I walked closer to the door and looked through the peephole, but it was covered, so I put the chain on it and pulled it open. "Emmitt?"

"Hey…" He said innocently.

"What are you doing here?"

"Can I come in please?" I closed the door to pull the chain from behind it. I was confused on how he even knew where I lived. I pulled the door opened and Emmitt walked in slowly. I backed up and he closed the door behind us and placed the chain back over it. Emmitt turned around and his eyes were bloodshot red.

"Emmitt what's wrong?"

"Do you love me Rose?"

"Of course I love you."

"Then why don't you want to be with me?" He walked toward me and I walked back. "We could move away from here and have another baby."

"Emmitt I just don't love you like that anymore and too much has happened."

"You know, your mother said something similar to me the night she was killed."

"Excuse me?"

"I just can't win with you Anderson women."

"Emmitt what are you talking about?" I said as I backed toward the kitchen. I had a feeling I might need to be close to a weapon.

Emmitt laughed. "Did you really think I broke up with you to play with college chicks?" He moved closer, "I can't do shit with a woman struggling the way I am. I like real women, women like your mother."

"Emmitt get the fuck out!"

"I can't do that Rose. I have to confess."

I was afraid now. My body shook and I dropped the blanket that I held around my body. I was done listening. I turned and ran for the kitchen butEmmitt grabbed me and tossed me back and I slid across the tiled floor and into the wall, cracking the sheetrock. Emmitt walked over to me and lifted me from the ground now with tears in his eyes. "I told her if I couldn't have her then no one could."

Snot dripped down my nose as I nodded my head in agreement to whatever he said in hopes that he would calm down and let me go.

"Now you making me do this shit again!"

"I'm not making you do anything."

"Yes you are! Do you even know the real reason we dated? It was your mother. She was so ashamed that she fell for a teenager. She made love to me and tossed me to the side telling me to find someone my own age, so I did her one better. I popped the cherry of her little daughter. She was my first and I was yours. You never forget your first Rose."

Tears started to roll down my cheeks. "Emmitt please let me go."

"You were all I had to remind me of her and what do you do? You start fucking bitches!" He yelled and saliva flew from his lips and speckled onto my face. "I tried to so hard to let you live your life. I really did, but instead of just fucking one you went and got another one. Never satisfied huh?" Emmitt snatched me buy my hair and drug me to the hall bathroom and turned on the water in the tub. "I guess we'll just have to make history repeat itself."

"Emmitt no!" I screamed and kicked.

"I have to thank you for making this easy. I already finished off Blaze, now I'll just kill you and the blame will fall on what's her name, Snitch? Snake?Oh yeah, Snapps."

I struggled more, but I could not get loose from his grip. I screamed help. I would not go down

223

without a fight. I closed my eyes and prayed to God for anything to happen that would get me away from Emmitt. He pulled me closer to the tub and I used all my strength to push him over, but he didn't budge. He lifted me up, but before he could get me completely off the floor I grabbed the scissors that poked out from the shave kit that used to belong to Snapps' father and cut out the wad of hair that he held. I jumped up and ran as fast as I could to the kitchen with him close behind. I grabbed a knife and turned around and Emmitt ran right into it. I pulled my hands back fast leaving the knife inside his flesh as he fell back. I fell down on the kitchen floor and broke into tears

"Rose!" I heard Snapps yell. "Rose take the chain off the door we need to talk."

I popped my head up and jumped up stepping over Emmitt's body and running to the door to let Snapps in. I threw my arms around her just happy to see her face. Snapps hugged me back and walked with me inside. She moved me to the side and walked over to check Emmitt's pulse. He was dead. I was shaking because I had never taken a life before, never even thought about it, but there was my first and the man who murdered my mother all wrapped into one lying on the floor. I was in so much pain. I just wanted everything to be over.

Snapps walked over to me to snap me out of a trance. She had come up with a way to clear the air. She ran outside to her car and wiped her prints from her gun and planted it on Emmitt, and then she dialed 911.

When the police finally arrived I told them everything that Emmitt said about murdering my mother and Blaze. I told them that he had been stalking me for months and devising a plan to hurt me and blame it on Snapps. I would not have lied otherwise, but after all I had done to Snapps the least I could do was keep her out of jail.

Snapps told the police that her gun had been missing a week before the initial incident with Blaze and that she was over at Lexi's when the attack happened. She told them that she fled the scene to follow Emmitt, but lost him during the chase.

We said whatever we could to make it all go away.

CHAPTER 21

Snapps

I had finally gotten a moment of peace after five days of nonstop questioning from the police and new reporters. I walked around my house grabbing everything that would fit into a dorm room. There was no way I was staying there after everything that happened. I was convinced that house was a bad omen, first my father passes a few weeks after it's purchased and then I almost kill somebody after me and the woman I thought loved me move in. I convinced my mother to put the house on the market and let someone else try their luck in it.

My grandmother had convinced my mom that it would be nice for me to live with her for a while since I had not seen them in years and I could go back to school and get a fresh start. My mom wanted to keep a tight grip on me after everything, but she knew she couldn't. I still needed to make my own decisions.

Lexi poked her head into the bathroom and I pulled down the shower curtain. "Yo, Rose just pulled up."

I turned to face Lexi then looked down at the ground.

"I can tell her to leave if you want."

"Nah, it's cool, you can let her in…"

"You sure?"

"Yeah…"

I resumed my position and pulled down the rest of the curtain. Moments later Rose was walking in. She didn't say a word, just stood in the doorway of the bathroom watching me.

"What are you doing here?" I asked since she wasn't going to say anything.

"I heard you were moving."

"Who told you that?"

"Your mom."

"When did you see her?"

"I stopped over by her first."

"Oh…" I turned to face Rose and noticed she was in all black. I already knew that meant she went to ole girl's funeral. It made me uneasy just knowing that, but there was nothing that I could say. We both stood silently for about a minute then Rose spoke. "Akeisha got arrested for shoplifting." She laughed softly.

"I'm not surprised."

"I'm sure it will be the first of many future crimes."

"Yeah, she might as well get comfortable in a cell."

We stood awkwardly in the bathroom again. It was as though there was nothing else to discuss, but that was a lie.

Rose cleared her throat then spoke, "Snapps I'm sorry…"

I bit my bottom lip at a loss for words.

Rose sighed, "I know those words probably mean absolutely nothing to you right now, but I mean them." she paused. "Would you look at me Snapps…please."

I looked up and my eyes watered.

"I never meant to hurt you or disrespect you. I made stupid decisions, I used you, I lied to you…"

Her words were knives through my heart, but they were the truth and I needed to hear them from her mouth.

"I can't justify anything that I did. All I know is that I was hurt from my mother passing and I was lost, but that is still no excuse because you were there for me no matter what," Rose began to choke on her words.

My body was shaking and I tried hard to contain the tears that wanted to fall. I just clenched my jaws and let her speak.

"It's like nobody was who they said they were, but you. I know you probably don't want to hear this, but even Blaze was a Snake," She laughed. "I went to her funeral and sat between two other girls she was dating at the same time as me." She paused again. "You asked me a question that day everything between you, me, and Blaze went down. You had tears in your eyes and you asked me was it worth it, was Blaze worth it."

I moved my hands to the inside of my pockets and stood silently still.

"The answer is no. I know that we didn't say this to each other often and it was probably mostly my fault, but I love you Snapps and I'm going to have to live with what I did every single day." Rose struggled to say then turned to walk out of the bathroom and out of my life forever. I removed my hands from my pockets and leaned over the sink broken as the tears finally flooded down my face.

Lexi walked in to check on me once Rose was gone. I waited for her to talk shit to me, but she didn't. She walked over to me and patted me on the back. "You good man?"

"I will be."

"Shit you better be and quick, all those fine ass women in Cali you about to be around."

I managed a smile and stood up straight. "I'm gonna miss you Lex."

"Aw don't come at me with the sentimental chick moments pretty boy." Lexi smiled. "You'll be home around the holidays so we can ball and I can get you lifted."

"You already know," Lexi and I bumped fist then hugged each other.

I packed up the rest of house and placed it on the back of the truck for storage then I locked the door and stood back to take one last look at what was soon to be my past. Lexi revved up the engine on the moving truck and I hopped into my car to put Rose and that house in my rearview. I connected my iPod to my radio and switched on B. Steady's starting over and I was on my way. No more Rose, Akeisha, or

Emmitt, no more drama. I was ready to live the life I should have been living from jump. I'd never let another woman cloud my vision again.

Other Titles By Christiana

GIRL
The Replacement Man
Tastebuds (Poetry)
Among Us
Intermission

Made in the USA
San Bernardino, CA
30 June 2016